"Okay, Seth. Let's Have This Out."

Samantha pushed up her sleeves. "Do you want me out of your hair?"

"I never said that."

"You don't have to be kind. It's your house. I'm the interloper. I can easily understand if you don't want me—" A poor choice of words, she realized instantly, because Seth's neck flushed red.

"I didn't say that, either."

It was her turn to hesitate. She couldn't pretend being unaware that she made him uncomfortable. And she could easily solve that problem by taking off. Although she was honestly fascinated with the ghost lore associated with the Connor house, Maine was peppered with colorful history. She could go somewhere else.

But if she was truthful—with herself—ghost lore was the last thing on her mind when she was with Seth.

Dear Reader,

We here at Silhouette Desire just couldn't resist bringing you another special theme month. Have you ever wondered what it is about our heroes that enables them to win the heroines' love? Of course, these men have undeniable sex appeal, and they have charm (loads of it!), and even if they're rough around the edges, you know that, deep down, they have tender hearts.

In a way, their magnetism, their charisma, is simply indescribable. These men are . . . simply Irresistible! This month, we think we've picked six heroes who are going to knock your socks off! And when these six irresistible men meet six *very* unattainable women, passion flares, sparks fly—and *you* get hours of reading pleasure!

And what month would be complete without a terrific *Man of the Month?* Delightful Dixie Browning has created a man to remember in Stone McCloud, the hero of *Lucy and the Stone. Man of the Month* fun just keeps on coming in upcoming months, with exciting love stories by Jackie Merritt, Joan Hohl, Barbara Boswell, Annette Broadrick, Lass Small and a *second* 1994 *Man of the Month* book by Ann Major.

So don't miss a single Silhouette Desire book! And, until next month, happy reading from . . .

Lucia Macro
Senior Editor

Please address questions and book requests to:
Reader Service
U.S.: P.O. Box 1325, Buffalo, NY 14269
Canadian: P.O. Box 1050, Niagara Falls, Ont. L2E 7G7

JENNIFER GREENE
BOTHERED

SILHOUETTE *Desire*

Published by Silhouette Books

America's Publisher of Contemporary Romance

SILHOUETTE BOOKS

ISBN 0-373-05855-1

BOTHERED

Copyright © 1994 by Jennifer Greene

Printed in U.S.A.

JENNIFER GREENE

lives near Lake Michigan with her husband and two children. Before writing full-time, she worked as a personnel manager, teacher and college counselor. Michigan State University honored her as an "outstanding woman graduate" for her work with women on campus.

Ms. Greene has written over thirty-five category romances for which she has won many awards, including the Rita for Best Short Contemporary book from Romance Writers of America and "Best Series Author" from *Romantic Times*.

To Meg Ruley

We've been together for more than forty books, and this dedication is long overdue. From the struggles through the good times, you've been there for me. I just want you to know that you're an unbeatable agent and an incomparable friend.

Thanks, Meg.

Prologue

Jock used the blade of his sword to lift the curtain at the third-story window. Below, a pickup truck pulled into the yard.

Jock watched with interest as the lad stepped out of the vehicle. Seth Connor, this one's name was. A few years over thirty in age, Jock guessed, and with the look of a fine, braw hell-raiser. Long limbs, a barrel chest and shoulders that would stuff a doorway—a man's man for certain.

Jock rubbed his hands together in anticipation. He'd have no trouble with this one. Helping the first Connor brother had been a touchy and difficult task; Zachary Connor had fought his efforts tooth and nail. But this one—Seth—was clearly different. Jock watched him wandering around below. The lad was as tall as a mountain, built healthy and strong, and he fair vibrated energy and virility with every step. He'd not let a woman push him around, that was for sure, but Jock would bet a doubloon that the lassies liked him. Only the saints knew why the men of the twentieth century favored short hair, but the lad's was chestnut brown, thick and curly—women always liked a bit of curl. The crinkle of humor in his eyes would draw the lassies, too; his skin was sunburnt to a handsome bronze and he had huge hands.

Jock could easily imagine those big hands on a woman. With a touch of luck, imagining would turn into reality before long. He already had the woman picked out for this one. The lass had been stopping at the house for a week now, knocking and peering in windows, clearly hoping to connect with the property owner.

Jock had already daydreamed about them connecting in the carnal sense. The sweet little thing was ripe for picking. Innocent eyes. A gentle, feminine way of moving. And the lass had a body that could even, and easily, arouse a ghost.

She'd bed like a dream, she would. Unless the lad were blind, he'd see it. Jock planned to watch every moment of the goings-on. Of course if Seth needed help with the seduction, he'd be there, but he was hard-pressed to believe that this one would need any instruction on *that* score. Clear as sunshine, Seth was a potently physical man. His shoulders and upper arms looked harder than hammered iron, and his face had the stamp of a man experienced in life. That sweet little darlin' of a lass was not likely to be much of a challenge for *him*.

Momentarily, though, Jock frowned. Below, Seth crossed around the front of the truck and yanked open the passenger door. Out leapt a big black mountain of a beast. Jock had never seen the like. The critter wasn't quite bear size, but close. Criminy. Jock hadn't anticipated having to tangle with a pet.

Still, no matter. He'd manage. The only problem that counted was connecting the lad with the gal, and sin couldn't be easier than that. The boy had virility and sexual prowess written all over him. He'd surely leap when he saw such easy prey as that soft-eyed little darling. He'd have her in his bed in a blink, Jock thought.

Again he rubbed his hands together gleefully.

Lar, this was going to be fun. For all his crimes, for all the black marks on his soul, Jock had always been good at one thing in his lifetime—and that was love. Arranging true love could be the tiniest bit tricky when the man and woman involved were unwilling, but that was surely not going to be a problem with these two. Both saint and sinner could see they were made for each other. There'd be no work, no trouble, no ghostly machinations required. He wouldna have a thing to do but watch . . . and enjoy.

From the moment Seth Connor crossed the threshold, he was one of Jock's boys.

One

What a place. The ocean at his doorstep. A round white lighthouse tucked in the lee of the cove, begging to be explored. The sun dappling a wild, rocky shoreline. A stand of tall, virgin pines curtaining the back property lines in privacy. And no woman in sight.

It was Seth Connor's idea of heaven.

He rolled his shoulders, trying to get the kinks out. He was a doer, not a sitter. Driving from Atlanta to Maine in a pickup with a slobbering one-hundred-and-fifty-pound Newfoundland had most definitely not been restful.

But they were here now. Seth sniffed the tangy salt air. In Georgia, the heat was already settling in by April. Here, the breeze blowing off the Atlantic was fresh and sassy, invigorating. Jezebel streaked past him in a blur of black fur. The pup was as antsy and full of pent-up energy as he was.

Digging the key from his jeans back pocket, he glanced at the house again. His younger brother Zach had already been here and described the place, so Seth knew ahead of time what she looked like. Still, Zach hadn't done the old baby justice. She was a regal three stories tall, white frame with dark green shutters and a widow's walk wrapped around the top story. Seth loved old things, and she looked like she'd weathered her share of storms over the generations. The basic architecture dated back to the 1700s, back when—in Seth's view—men had the sense to build things to last. The house had the look of character and endurance, and he valued both. His brother never really described the beauty of the place—probably because Zach was so determined to warn him that he was going to find a mystery in the house.

That idea still made Seth chuckle. His youngest brother was a brilliant musician and creative to the bone, but definitely not grounded in reality the way he was. Sure, there was a mystery. None of the three brothers knew why their grandfather had owned this big old albatross to begin with—they all suspected he must have kept a woman here—but with Gramps gone, they'd probably never know the answer to that. The problem on their table was far more practical than "mysterious." Somehow they had to get rid of their unexpected and totally unmanageable inheritance. Zach had come here six months ago to get a sale in motion. He'd become totally distracted from that goal when he fell in love.

The chances of that problem happening to him, Seth figured, were about five thousand to one.

Great odds.

He whistled. Jezebel promptly bounded to his side, her pink tongue lolling and her tail wagging at gale force. "Come on, girl. Let's check out the inside." A tarp covered his carpenter tools and gear in the truck bed. He untied the rope, grabbed his canvas tote and a twenty-pound bag of dog food and trekked for the front porch. Juggling the load, he managed to fit the key and turn it. The heavy oak door swung open.

He had a thirty-second glimpse of a cave-sized hall and an open mahogany staircase, but that was it. Jezebel, out of the clear blue, suddenly freaked. She took one sniff inside, lifted her big black head in the air and howled. Worse, she tried to climb all over him at the same time. The sack of dog food thumped to the ground as Seth struggled to keep his balance. The sack split open. Bits of dog chow scattered everywhere.

"Would you cut it out? Behave yourself. Sit. I said *sit.*" The firm, authoritative command was as worthless as last week's newspaper. The dog knocked the canvas tote right out of his hand, baying louder than a wounded wolf.

Seth sighed. Jezebel was the only female he trusted...but there was no denying that she was a hopeless wuss. He'd bought the pup when Gail left him. At six weeks old, the dog had been an irresistible sixteen pounds of fluff and easy to spoil. Too easy. She was almost a year old now, and it was his own damn fault he had a lapdog the size of an Angus cow. He dropped down on a level with her, ducking away from her frantic wet kisses, playing with her as he tried to stroke and soothe.

"What are you scared of, huh? It's just a house, doofus. There'll be fresh food and water in there.

Cookies. Nothing to be afraid of. The biggest live thing you could possibly run across in there is a mouse. You know how much bigger you are than a mouse? And to think I almost named you Killer. Get *off* me, you big lummox. If you think you're sitting on my lap for the rest of the afternoon, you're out of your mind. Your ancestors saved people's lives. I've told you a hundred times. Newfoundlands are known for their courage, so how come you're such a gutless wonder? Could you try to calm down, you big baby? Could you at least *try?*''

"She's . . . um . . . quite a dog.''

The sound of a feminine voice startled him. Seth hadn't heard any car drive up, although when he whipped his head around, the vehicle was clearly visible. The dusty red Firebird was parked right behind his truck. He could see the tail end of the sports car, from the open space between her legs.

She had an unforgettable pair of long, bare legs. Seth didn't mind that view, but he hadn't planned on encountering a woman. If he had, he'd have chosen to be upright, not lying flat with a one-hundred-and-fifty-pound rug rat draped on his chest and lavishing his face with embarrassing doggie kisses. His posture lacked all dignity. One look at the woman, and Seth wanted all the dignity he could beg, borrow or steal.

Jezebel, of course, promptly forgot whatever she'd been afraid of and jammed a paw in his ribs on a pivot. Swishing her fat tail in his face, she barreled straight for the stranger. A new human. A new sucker to con. Jezzie always acted around strangers as if she were desperately deprived of attention and no one had ever loved her.

Unfortunately the lady had no way to know that Jezzie was harmless. Even people familiar with big dogs had been known to hightail it to the nearest rooftop when Jezebel aimed for them at a full gallop. The pup had the concept of acceleration down pat, but she hadn't mastered braking quite as well. Seth anticipated a scared-witless feminine shriek of terror.

"Jezzie! *Stay!*" he yelled out, and then on the sink of a breath muttered, "Aw, hell." It could have been worse. At least Jezzie hadn't mowed her down, and the stranger was distinctly chuckling instead of screaming. Damn. Seth wiped a hand over his face, mortified to see the slime trail of a tongue dampening the sleeve of her blouse. "I'm real sorry about that."

"No sweat. I don't mind."

Truthfully she didn't seem to. She scratched Jezzie behind the ears, which was all it took to transfer his dog's loyalty. The pup promptly sat on her foot, raised newly adoring eyes to the stranger—what Seth called her sucking-up posture—and accepted the petting as her due.

"Real watchdog, hmm?"

"Bred for killer instincts," he said gravely.

"I can see that. No burglar would ever get by you, would they, sweetie pie? You'd lick them to death. I'll bet the only thing you know how to attack is food. Why, you're just an overgrown baby, aren't you, precious..."

Seth had never figured out what made fully grown adults baby-talk to animals, and right then he didn't much care. While she crooned sweet nothings to Jezzie, he had the chance to lurch to a sitting position—and get a serious look at his visitor. Wariness instantly shot to his pulse.

The long legs he'd already noticed. A monk in a monastery would be hard pressed to ignore those. Seth had no particular religious calling, but he'd recently adopted a monk's celibate life-style. She was all the reasons why.

Technically she was dressed simply—sandals, a khaki skirt, a loose safari-print blouse. Nothing outright suggestive. But the skirt was short and snug and made no secret that she had a damn cute tush. She'd also opted for no bra. Her blouse was a dark print and oversized—nothing showed, no reason on earth she needed to truss herself up in a corset, only the fretful spring breeze plastered the fabric against her firm, full breasts as explicitly as a lover's palms. Her open-toed sandals revealed scarlet painted toenails. A chunk of crystal dangled from a gold chain on her neck, raw crystal, not like formal jewelry but more like an occult love charm or talisman, and destined to catch a man's eye where it rested in the delectable hollow between her breasts. The sun caught the light in the crystal, turned it into jewels and rainbow prisms. A guy might notice this effect, if he could tear his eyes off her body.

Seth tore his eyes off her body, but the view above the neck was no less dangerous. Her hair was a dark rich sable, rippling past her shoulders, worn straight and smooth Cleopatra style. Her nose was too long, her chin too square to rate a classic label of beauty, but everything about her face was striking. Gypsy-dark eyes, deep set and almond shaped, were accented by skin softer than a baby's rump and sharp, high cheekbones blushed with sun.

At first glance, her eyes had a softness, a sweetness, that made him think of innocence. Seth bought that like a politician's promises. He guessed her age as late twenties. No crow's feet or wrinkles yet, but the way she walked and moved, she'd long discovered that she liked being a woman, knew the allure she had for men and liked that, too. She was about five feet five inches, maybe one hundred and fifteen pounds, every one of them packed with sexual dynamite. Her lush, full mouth had a glossy tint of scarlet—no surprise— and her lips were curved in a grin full of mischief.

Seth gave her fifty brownie points for liking his dog. Nobody who liked dogs was all bad. But he hoped she'd stopped for something innocuous like asking directions, because the dance of mischief in her eyes made him real, real nervous.

While Jezebel slavishly, lavishly washed her hand, she was looking him over, too.

That made him more nervous.

"I've been trying for days to connect with the owner of this house," she said cheerfully. "Are you one of the Connors?"

Since his gear was strewn all over the porch, it would sound pretty hoaxy to deny it. "Yeah. Seth Connor. How'd you know the name?"

"I've been studying the history of certain houses down the coast. Yours was of special interest. A man in town—Rolf Gerlain, the guy who runs a corner grocery—told me that the house had been in the Connor family for a couple of generations now. Truthfully I'm interested in the time period before that, but I could never seem to find anyone home to ask."

"I just got here," Seth admitted.

"And you're not from Maine." She chuckled at his look of surprise. "That wasn't hard to guess. You have a Southern drawl. I'd bet . . . Georgia?"

She guessed right. He couldn't pin down her background from her accent quite that easily, but he'd bet East Coast and old money. More relevant, her voice had a husky burr that was going to make any man fantasize about hot summer nights and long, lazy sex. He hoped she left soon.

Unfortunately that didn't appear to be her immediate plan. She seemed to have decided that formal introductions were in order. With Jezzie trailing her like a shadow, she aimed straight toward him with a hand extended. The bangle bracelet on her wrist glittered in the sun. In the shade of the porch, he could smell her perfume. Nothing strong, but distinctively spicy. Exotic and erotic, just like her. "My name is Samantha. Samantha Adams. And I'm really glad to meet you, Seth."

Hell, he had to give her brownie points for the handshake too. Firm, straightforward, quick. Just long enough for him to feel her pampered palm and the slight dampness of feminine nerves. Vulnerable, Seth thought, and immediately found his protective instincts aroused. Not for her. For him.

He'd fallen for the illusion of vulnerability before, and ended up with a kick below the belt. When a man was kicked hard enough, Seth followed the philosophy that a guy should have the good sense to stay down. He dropped her hand. Quickly.

"Pleased to meet you, too." The courtesy lie was unavoidable. In Georgia a man could murder, steal and lie just like anywhere else, but he was expected to show manners around a lady. Still, Seth didn't figure there was any rule against tactfully prodding her along. "I'm afraid I still don't quite understand why you're here."

"I know. I should have said right away. But heavens, I'm afraid this is going to sound a little nuts, coming from a stranger." She hesitated with a charming smile, doubtless intended to make her look as trustworthy as a Girl Scout. No sale. There was no question that she was adorable, if a guy was attracted to dangerous substances, but she'd never manage a Girl Scout look even with ten pounds of merit badges pinned to her chest. Not *that* chest. "I was wondering if there was any chance you might let me study your house."

"Study? This house? What kind of study?"

She hesitated again. "When I drove up, it looked as if your dog was afraid to go inside."

"Jezebel's afraid of her own shadow. She's a born coward." Seth didn't get the connection between his dog's behavior and her interest in the house.

"Maybe she had a reason to be afraid. Animals have always been particularly sensitive to psychic phenomena."

"Psychic phenomena," Seth echoed. He took another look at the crystal and the bangles and the gypsy-dark eyes. Aw, hell, he thought, the clues had been there. He'd just been so busy worrying about her sex appeal that it hadn't occurred to him that she was a kook. A new-age, crystal-channeling, reincarnation-believing type of kook.

"There's quite a bit of evidence that your house has some really special history. That's what I've been studying. Houses down the coast of Maine that have a psychic background. Possibly your Jezebel was afraid of a ghost."

"I'm sure," Seth said kindly, and lurched to his feet. "Look, I just got here. I haven't even settled in yet. I hope you have real good luck with your psychic research and all, but—"

"But you think ghosts are nonsense? You don't have to say it. I can see from your expression. And I can't tell you how much that relieves my mind." Her smile was as potent as pure liquid sunshine. "I mean . . . I honestly wasn't sure how to handle this. I was worried about telling you. Some people could react by really being afraid if they knew their house had a history of being haunted."

"Trust me. You didn't need to be worried." A massive understatement, Seth thought.

"Then you wouldn't mind if I came in?"

"Pardon?"

"Inside. Your house. Actually what I'd like to do is an extensive study that would take some time. But even if I just walked in, I could see if I could pick up any . . . vibrations. Feelings. I mean, maybe there's nothing there—at least nothing I could work with, in which case I'd just be wasting my time and yours, too. But I won't know that unless I try. You wouldn't mind if I just walked through for a minute, would you?"

Seth paused. He wasn't afraid of ghosts. He also didn't particularly care if a herd of strangers tromped through the house—they would, soon enough, in the process of trying to sell it. He didn't know what was in there, but positively there was nothing personal of his, so it wasn't as if she would be intruding on any private territory. And granted, she was a teensy bit pushy and a tad eccentric, but Seth sincerely doubted she was going to turn into a raving psychopath if he let her inside. Hell, he could just oust her if she did. She was no pint-size elf, but at six-two and a solid two hundred pounds, he had no doubts about his ability to handle any physical situation.

Still, there was no way this side of Poughkeepsie he wanted her in the house—or anywhere near him. It had nothing to do with a fear of ghosts. It had do with her dark, sloe eyes. It had to do with the female sexuality she exuded from every pore. It had to do with her long slim legs and that tight little rump.

Since Gail, he'd had the good sense to avoid the kind of woman who tempted his hormones. Not that his libido was racing rampant at the idea of becoming involved with a kook. But caution, Seth had discovered, could protect a man better than a heavy artillery Uzi. He didn't need another kick in the ego. He didn't put himself in the position, not anymore, where there was even a slim chance of him failing.

"Seth—?" Apparently he'd been quiet too long. She was still waiting for an answer.

"Sorry. And I don't want to seem rude, but I have to be honest. The answer is no."

Two

He really hadn't wanted her inside, Samantha thought.

Thankfully his Newfoundland had come to her rescue. Jezebel had clamped wolflike teeth on her wrist—swallowing her entire hand in the process—and looked at her owner with big yearning eyes. *Isn't she a great new toy? Can't we keep her?* Seth hadn't budged for the pup, but he'd let out an exasperated, embarrassed sigh at the look of dog drool on her blouse and hand. Since he hadn't been in the house, he had no idea where the kitchen or bathrooms were located, but there was surely a sink somewhere. He couldn't very well deny her the chance to clean up.

As meek as a lamb, her head ducked in the submissive posture of a nun, Samantha had zoomed past him through the front door.

So far she hadn't gotten any farther than that—and didn't need to. Any thought of washing her hands fled from her mind. She could do that any old time, and heavens. From her first step inside, she was in love.

She'd already read about the house, of course. But gleaning knowledge from the printed page could hardly compare with the experience of really seeing it. An open staircase, split in two sets of stairs, dominated the long shadowy hall. The staircase was far more narrow than the one where Rhett had carried Scarlett upstairs, but Samantha's imagination was flexible. She easily adjusted for eighteenth-century architecture, substituted a pirate for Rhett, and envisioned herself being carried—kicking and screaming, of course—straight to the wicked-ravisher-of-a-pirate's bed.

She spun around. A brass chandelier, as wide as a man, hung from the ceiling and caught the wink of pale sunlight from a round window above. The window was leaded glass. Through an open door she glimpsed an octagonal-shaped turret room, reminiscent of princesses and fairy tales, and through another door she saw the rough fieldstone of an ancient, ceiling-tall fireplace and hearth.

Seth Connor dropped a canvas suitcase behind her. It hit the wooden floor with a decidedly practical plunk. "I don't know where the kitchen or bathrooms are. You're on your own."

"Hmm. No problem."

He disappeared outside, then came back in carting a sack of dog food on his shoulder, heading downstream in the long river of a hall. "The kitchen's in here," he called a moment later.

"Thanks so much," she called back, but she never moved. There was no way she could stop looking. Arched doors led off both sides of the hall. A huge oval mirror framed in ornate gold hung at the far end. The most exciting thing, though, was the distinctive draught of cold air near the base of the stairs. The draft was enough to chase a delicious shiver up Samantha's spine. Jezebel must have sensed it, too, because when the dog ventured that far inside, she promptly erupted in a cacophony of growls and barks.

The sound brought Seth hustling out of the kitchen. "For cripes sake, cut it out, Jezzie. You're going straight outside if you can't behave."

"Honestly, it's not her fault," Samantha said over the high-pitched howls. "I think she senses a ghost."

"And cats fly," Seth muttered. He yanked the oak front door open. Jezebel peeled out like a bee was on her tail.

"She won't run too far and get lost?"

"Jezzie's a couch potato. Hell, she won't even walk unless I go with her. She's never let me out of her sight yet. Her getting lost is *not* a problem."

She was, his tone implied.

At that precise moment, it seemed a politically good idea to remove her troublesome body from his sight. "I'll just go find a powder room," Samantha said judiciously, trying to imply that she'd leave instantly after that. He looked relieved.

She could hardly explore further under the circumstances, but she managed to poke her head in three rooms before discovering a charmingly outmoded bathroom with a pull chain john and a pedestal porcelain sink. A fresh bar of pear soap rested on a Victorian saucer, but she found no towels. After washing her hands, she shook them until they were dry enough, and then ducked back into the hall.

As she'd hoped, her short absence had made him forget about her. He seemed to have forgotten about unpacking and settling in, too. Leaning against a doorjamb, she watched Seth run his hands over the peeling wainscotting, knock on walls for hollow spots, bend down to examine the grain on the hardwood floor. His brow was furrowed in concentration. He didn't seem to notice she was there.

God, he was adorable. Not precisely handsome, Samantha mused. She'd grown up around legions of pin-striped, cultured, well-educated males who qualified as formally handsome. Seth was towering tall and built lean and mean. The sleeves of his black T-shirt could barely accommodate his muscular forearms and lumberjack shoulders. The jeans molding his long angular legs had never seen a designer label. They were a pale blue from years of washing and wear, and they fit his flat behind with the faithfulness of an old friend. His hands could span her waist and have room left over.

Samantha bet he could hold his own in a dark alley with anyone. More relevant, she'd love to know how he stripped—he couldn't possibly be *that* good-looking without clothes, could he? But the mischievously wicked thought didn't linger in her mind long.

It was his face that snared her attention. His dusty brown hair was brushed back and clipped short, accenting the strong angular bones of his face. His skin had a natural burn from sun and wind; experience had carved character lines around his eyes and brow; and his eyes were a shrewd, sharp blue.

There was something in his eyes that made her heart slow down, slow *way* down, as if she'd been running for a long time and finally found a place to rest. She wasn't sure where that feeling came from. Maybe it was from his incomparable gentleness with his massively overgrown pup; maybe it was noticing the bruised shadows under his eyes or the straight-shooter way he looked at her. Samantha couldn't remember trusting a man on sight—lessons in life had obliterated that kind of naïveté years ago—so her draw to Seth was rare. Equally rare was the way his shiver-low masculine tenor aroused every feminine nerve in her body.

"You're still here."

Oops. It appeared he'd noticed her after all. And those deep blue eyes certainly packed enough sexual voltage to make a woman's heart thump, but Samantha suspected he did that just breathing. Her fascination with him was regrettably one-sided. From his tone of voice, there wasn't much question that she was as popular as a tick on a hound. "I really didn't mean to bother you. I'll get out of your way," she said.

Her tone dripped embarrassment and remorse. It wasn't often she used such ruthless feminine tactics, but Samantha had to admit they worked like a charm. He promptly hesitated, looking as guilty as if he'd accidentally kicked a kitten. "Hell, I didn't mean to be rude. It's just that I've been on the road for two days, only pulled in here an hour ago. There are so many things to do around here that I don't even know where to start."

"And then a total stranger barges in on you, the last thing you needed? I'm sorry, honestly. I really didn't know you were just arriving after a long trip."

"Yeah, well, you had no way to know that." He hesitated again, his gaze lanced on her face as if pulled by a magnet. He only looked for seconds before breaking the contact. Lurching to his feet, he dug a tape measure out of his back pocket. "You don't really believe in that kind of thing, do you? Ghosts, spirits and all that?"

"I have no idea," she admitted cheerfully. That answer seemed to startle him, and darned if she knew why he was measuring the long hall, but she promptly jogged to the far end to hold the tape. When he crouched down, she crouched down.

"I thought you said you were studying psychic stuff like that."

"I am." Heavens, she thought, he was actually volunteering to have a conversation. She was more than willing to oblige. "I have an aunt—Frances—who loves anything to do with the occult. Instead of giving me dolls at Christmas, she used to give me Ouija boards, history books on ghosts and reincarnation, the *I Ching,* that kind of thing. Anyway. She really believes you can make a connection after someone dies, and she exposed me to all this 'evidence'... I mean, people from every race and culture have believed in ghosts from the beginning of time. So I caught the curiosity bug. Figured I'd spend six months studying it for myself."

"Yeah?" When he stood up with a frown, she stood up too. The tape measure rolled back with a snap. As far as she could tell, he was concentrating on nothing but his measurements. "So... you've been at it how long now?"

"Since around the first of March."

"And have you managed to make . . . um . . . one of those connections?"

"Nope."

Seth rolled his eyes. "But you've still kept at it? You must have a pretty unusual job, if you can take off half a year like that."

Apparently they were measuring wainscotting now. She had the job of holding the tape measure down pat. "Actually I saved up to do it. I wasn't exactly leaving a career. I mean—I've always worked. Everything from waiting tables to being a lawyer's secretary to ladling out food in a soup kitchen for the homeless. I worked in a library for a while, spent two years putting together fund-raisers for a charity organization."

He must not have liked the width of the wainscotting, either, because he frowned again. Not at her. Just at the wall. He seemed to be making a concerted effort to avoid looking directly at her. "Sounds like you've got quite a résumé for someone who doesn't look over twenty five."

"Twenty-seven."

"Hmm. So . . . if I've got this right . . . you just took off for six months. To see if you could personally meet up with some ghosts. Concentrating, apparently, on whatever garden variety of spirit might be haunting the Maine coastline?"

His voice was so deadpan that she had to resist the urge to laugh. She could have told him there were other reasons she'd left home for six months, reasons not so frivolous or flighty, but this was more fun. He clearly thought her ghost project was worth a hill of beans, but there was an unholy gleam of humor in his eyes—fine, dry humor—that warmed her from the inside out. Did he even know how naturally he was teasing her?

"There was a reason I picked Maine," she responded. "My home is Philadelphia, but my family have a vacation place in Kennebunkport. So I knew this area—we spent every summer in Maine—and my aunt filled me in on a dozen 'haunting sites' down the coast."

"How helpful of her," he murmured wryly. "So that's where you're set up? Your family's place?"

"No. Actually I'm not living anywhere. At the moment, I'm just tent camping in Acadia. Your house was an easy drive from the park. Naturally I didn't know if I was going to be able to connect with you, but I was close enough there to give it a good shot. I've had a list of houses up and down the coast that I wanted to study, so I've just camped wherever they were. There was an incredible place outside of Brendel, an old seventeenth-century inn—"

"You're *tent* camping?" he interrupted her. Apparently they were all through measuring things. The tape measure dangled from his hand like a dead snake. A forgotten dead snake. His attention, most suddenly, was focused all on her. "That little Firebird couldn't pack anything more substantial than a pup tent."

"It doesn't. That's what I have—a pup tent."

"This time of year, it has to get pretty chipper at night."

"Cold enough. I've wakened up a few mornings thinking my toes were ice cubes," she said with a grin.

"A lot of people around the park?"

"Actually there's hardly a soul. It's nice and quiet. Private."

"Then you're alone? By yourself? In the wild like that?"

Why, the darling was worried about her, Samantha realized. She was charmed. For a short stretch, she'd had the impossibly illogical sensation that he was afraid of her. Obviously that was silly; Seth was a strapping strong man who had no reason to be afraid of anything or anyone. Still, she'd never had a man look at her with such caution and wariness—although Seth couldn't know it, that was a real treat—and she'd truly never anticipated finding an old-fashioned protective white knight beneath those shrewd blue eyes.

Her smile danced across her face slowly. "Women camp alone all the time these days," she said gently. "Even if they didn't, believe me, it's not a problem. I can take care of myself."

A streak of lightning lit up the black sky, illuminating the wild froth of silver waves way out over the Atlantic. Jezebel fretfully nuzzled her head under his palm. "Take it easy, babe. The heart of the storm's miles away. At most we're gonna get a little rain. Nothing to get nervous about." Seth automatically soothed the dog, but his eyes were peering out the second-story window to the lawn in the distance.

There was a pup tent down there. Parked right on his front lawn. Presumably Samantha Adams was in it and sound asleep, since there wasn't a sign of light or life anywhere around it.

Damned if he knew how she'd ended up there. Yeah, he'd invited her, but it was the "how" that still had him bewildered. Seth had a woman carpenter in his employ. He'd never tended toward chauvinism, never fathomed how some guys got defensive around strong women, never thought there were things the female gender couldn't or shouldn't do.

Only Samantha was different than any other woman he knew. First she'd started rattling all that ditsy stuff about ghosts, and then she'd gone on about her job-hopping history. She wasn't a lightweight—hell, there was plenty of intelligence in her eyes—but it was frighteningly obvious to Seth that she was as flighty as a bird, no more grounded than a buttercup in the wind. *Naturally* he'd freaked out at the idea of her camping alone in the wilderness. Anything could happen to her. Animals. Men. Weather. She was so damned pretty that she was bound to attract preda-tors, and it wasn't as if he cared if she wanted to stick around and study *ghosts* for a few days. She didn't seem to have a practical, sensible bone in her whole body, and it bothered him, the idea of her freezing that cute little tush in a flimsy pup tent with no protec-tion....

A fat blop of rain splatted on the window. Then another one, then a whole slew of big, plump crys-tally drops. Resolutely Seth turned away. It wasn't his problem if she got wet. He'd done more than most men would volunteer under the circumstances. She was as safe as a nun in a convent on his front lawn; nobody was going to bother her there. No way, no how, did he need to feel any more responsible for her than that.

Jezebel shadowed his side as he stalked downstairs. He'd already explored the parameters of the house. Easier than the snap of his fingers, he forgot Saman-tha and concentrated on the projects ahead.

It wasn't often he could do something to help his brothers. The oldest Connor, Michael, was a business prodigy and brain. His youngest brother, Zach, had been born creative, destined to be a success in the music world.

Seth had always felt like a misfit. The ordinary brother. No special talents, no special brilliance. He did okay as a carpenter, had four people working for him full-time now, but the truth was, he was easily satisfied. He had to be his own boss, needed to get out in the air and not be cooped up all day, but he'd never wanted to do anything but work with his hands. He loved building, loved fixing things, loved working with wood. But there'd never been a thing he could do to really help his brothers. Until now.

The house was a paradise for a carpenter who loved old things and restoration work. They had to sell the place, of course. None of them had any ties in Maine, no possible use for an albatross of a white elephant in this neck of the country. But Seth could sure as hell increase its selling price with a little work.

He wandered around, making lists and plans in his head. The hardwood floors—especially the precious chestnut floors—needed sanding, planing, varnishing. Someone had mistakenly painted the kitchen cupboards; a little strip job, and he'd have them back to natural oak in no time. Upstairs, the blue and green bedrooms at the far end were pip-squeak size, with no bearing wall between them. If he ripped out the wall, he could make one sweetie of an upstairs TV/game/media room to relax in.

He was completely concentrating on the house, so damned if he knew how he ended up standing in front of an east window again. Damn storm should have moved east, just like any other normal weather pattern. Instead it seemed to be moving in. The rain had turned into serious business, sluicing down the glass panes in steady rivulets. The grass was soaking it in, glistening under the black sky like a sponge of diamonds. Jezebel whined, nuzzling in front of him for a view.

"Yeah, she's still there. And apparently sleeping like a baby. You don't see any sign of life, do you? If there was anything wrong, she'd be moving around. For cripes sake, would you settle *down*. She's not our problem, doofus. Just forget about her. I swear you're as restless as a caged cat."

So was he. Seth jammed a hand through his hair, and abruptly decided he'd call his brother. It was almost eleven, but Michael was a chronic insomniac, so there was no fear of waking him up, and Seth wanted to discuss his plans for the house.

The nearest telephone was in the kitchen, an old fashioned black model with a circular dial. As expected, Michael was up and wide-awake, and heard him out before asking, "Are you sure you've got the time to do all that?"

"It won't take me that long. A few weeks, at most a month. I really think some surface improvements would update the place, increase the value before we put it on the market. And I've got Stitch covering for me at home. Nothing he can't handle while I'm away." Seth didn't say that being far away from Atlanta—and Gail—would surely act like a shot of penicillin for the moody blues he'd been plagued with. "Are you doing okay?"

"Sure. Just busy."

His brother sounded tired. Seth hesitated, wanting to ask how he was *really* doing. Michael had closed up like a clam after Carla left him. Everything was always "fine," as if the sudden severing of a ten-year-old marriage was no big thing. Seth suspected otherwise, but what could he say? They were close—hell, if one of his brothers needed him, Seth would have torn down a mountain to get there—but the Connor men had a history of bad luck with women that went back generations. It was a touchy subject at best, and since he sure as petunias didn't want to be grilled about Gail, he couldn't very well press Michael to talk about his ex-wife.

Michael solved the problem by changing the subject to the one Connor brother who'd broken the pattern. "Have you talked to Zach?"

"Just a few hours ago."

"Did he tell you his new bride was pregnant?"

Seth chuckled. "Yeah, and from what I hear, Kirstin's doing fine. He's got morning sickness pretty bad. She's hoping that he'll be obliging and go into labor for her, too."

Michael laughed, making Seth feel good. When he hung up the phone, he still felt good . . . until he realized that he'd been talking with the phone cord stretched its full length to the doorway. Through the door was a view of the hall. Past the hall was an open door to an old fashioned parlor/living room. From which, if he craned his neck like an ostrich, he could see the tail end of a wet pup tent through the far window.

"Jezebel," he snapped, "we're going to bed. For cripes sake, it's nearly midnight."

He unwound the phone cord, clapped the receiver back on the hook and then—muttering under his breath—went on a search mission for the rabbit. Damned dog looked perfectly ridiculous carrying around a stuffed animal, but she wouldn't sleep without it. Once Jezzie had the toy, she pelted straight upstairs.

Seth started to. On the fifth step up, he heard a crack of thunder that shook the house. He stopped, then set his mouth in a firm line and trudged the rest of the way up. Halfway through the hall, he peeled off his black T-shirt. Once inside the master bedroom, he pulled off his work boots with a baleful glance at the silent lump on the bed.

"Did you think I wouldn't notice you, you big galoot? And I'll grant you, babe, you're the only female I'd even consider sleeping with. But I'm not that desperate yet. And you snore. Down. I mean it, now."

Jezebel thumped down with the earless white rabbit in her mouth, and settled in a behemoth-sized heap at the foot of the bed. Seth unbuttoned the top snap of his jeans, avoiding the view from the window as if it would bite him. The decor in the master bedroom was distracting enough to divert any man's attention.

If his grandfather had decorated the sucker, Seth couldn't help but wonder at the old reprobate's sex life. Red velvet drapes hung from the French doors and windows. The four-poster bed was set on a platform, sultan style. The furnishings were fine antiques—really fine, like the zebra wood chiffonier—but Seth could hardly fail to notice the cornerstone fireplace, the plush Persian rugs, the sin-red lounging chaise. The whole thing was a seducer's lair. How a celibate guy was supposed to sleep in a room that reeked of sensual pleasures was beyond him. Hell's bells, the room was made for sex.

He flicked off the light. And yawned. Nothing dangerous about the room in the dark, and driving for two solid days had exhausted him. He was beat. He'd sleep just fine.

He headed straight for the bed. At least he took three steps in that direction. Somehow—he never planned it—his feet seemed determined to take a detour route past the window.

Below, it was raining cats and dogs.

The pup tent looked soaked through, water running down the peaked edge like a river. Seth scratched his chest, his brow pitched in a growl of a frown. There was no reason to worry about her. None. If the tent leaked—if she was wet or in trouble—she'd obviously have the practical good sense to come to the front door, wouldn't she? She *had* to have that much of a brain.

With no sweat at all, he recalled her sweet husky voice when she'd been baby-talking to Jezzie. He remembered the irrepressible humor in her dark sloe eyes, the look of her ripe full breasts straining against her blouse, the tuck of her fanny when she'd crouched down, the way her sable-thick hair swished around her shoulders when she moved. He remembered her mouth. He remembered her long white throat. He remembered her legs.

The clarity of those recollections was no surprise. Samantha Adams was the kind of woman that no man was likely to forget. Especially him. Seth had developed some fine-honed ducking tactics around certain women. Samantha might as well have a tattoo spelling trouble on her forehead. It wasn't a problem. He wasn't going near her. It was just that—to save his life—he couldn't dredge up a single memory that made him believe she had a lick of practical common sense.

The windows and doors were all closed. Even so, he could hear the waves pounding on the rocky shore. The wind had picked up, swirling dust and debris in the air, and the rain was now coming down in torrents.

A splintering crack of lightning suddenly pierced the sky. So close that Seth muttered a swear word. Seconds later, the groan and growl of thunder shook the whole house.

He swore again. Loudly.

And took off downstairs.

Three

Samantha loved to sleep. Her mother used to claim that she could sleep through an elephant stampede. She'd thankfully never had the chance to test that premise, but storms were positively her favorite sleeping weather. A good, dark, drenching downpour was an excuse to snuggle down and let her imagination race along the extravagant lines of erotic adventures and exotic fantasies.

She replayed the best ones from storm to storm.

Even her wildest, kinkiest dreams, though, had never before included a dog with a black wet nose nuzzling her bare foot. The man next to the dog fit more naturally into the fantasy. She knew who he was. Seth. He'd already been wandering around her dream, stripped down to stark naked, doing unspeakably delicious things to her body that she would certainly never let a man do outside of a dream, but hey, a fantasy was a fantasy. Only this fantasy had developed a surprising plot twist, because Seth was suddenly miraculously dressed, his hair soaking wet and dripping, and his forehead pinched in an exasperated frown.

"Hmm?" she murmured.

"My Lord. It's like trying to wake the dead. You can't stay out here. The storm's moving in."

Samantha heard it. She was just confused for a moment. The dog's face, peering through the tent flap, was certainly real. But the sound of pounding waves and growly thunder had been part of her dream, and so had the sweet hiss of rain. He'd been seducing her in the wet grass, as she recalled. It had been a heck of a wild night, and a heck of a wild ride...

"The lightning is too close. It's dangerous out here. You have to come in the house."

"Hmm?"

"Look, I know you don't know me and I'm sure the idea makes you nervous, but there's nothing for you to worry about. I mean, take one look at the weather and you'll know I'm only talking common sense. If you want to find a motel, that's fine, but it's the middle of the night. I have no idea where a motel is, and it's not like the house doesn't have a half dozen bedrooms upstairs. None of the beds are made up, but you've already got a sleeping bag, and I...damn. Are you awake or not?"

"Sure," she murmured groggily. With a noisy yawn, she maneuvered around in the sleeping bag enough to sit up, but her eyes promptly closed again. The sound of the ocean reminded her of another fantasy involving water. "I don't suppose you ever saw the movie *Charade?* There's this scene where Cary Grant and

Audrey Hepburn are on a boat in Paris. He's been fighting this passionate attraction for her all this time, but then she kisses him, and he says, 'Honey, when you come on ... you come *on*.' That scene *still* sends tingles down my spine."

There was a moment's silence. Then a low masculine mutter. "It's raining cats and dogs, lightning close enough to fry us both and she's talking *tingles* down her spine." A large, flat hand started patting around in the darkness. "I think she's missing a piston, Jezzie. Looks like we're on our own, but she has to have a jacket and shoes around here somewhere."

"Afraid I sleep awfully heavily," she confessed.

"No kidding."

"But I'm awake now."

"Yeah? And I believed in the tooth fairy. Until I was six. Lift your arm, Ms. Adams. You can do that much, can't you?"

She could. Still muttering, he threaded her arms through the sleeves of her jacket, then flopped the fabric over her head and across her shoulders. He nearly smothered her in the process. It was dark. The pup tent was ample size for her, but add a huge man crawling on his knees and a bear-size dog determined not to be left out, and injury was inevitable. A paw the size of a tree trunk pinned her foot. An elbow nearly collided with her nose. Her sleeping bag was unzipped—she always slept with it open—but so much weight pressed on it from different directions that she couldn't possibly move.

She started giggling.

"The lady thinks this is funny? The tent's gonna collapse, the sky's threatening Armageddon, damned if I can find her shoes, and she starts laughing, Jez. You have any ideas what we should do with her?''

"I appreciate your help. I really do. It's really kind of you—I didn't realize how bad the weather was.'' She tried to choke back another chuckle, but it pealed out anyway.

"For cripes sake, Jezebel, no wonder I couldn't find that shoe. Drop it.''

"I also appreciate your offer to stay in the house—''

"*Drop* it, you big lummox.''

"But I'm awake now. I promise. And I think there's a teensy chance we'd all get out of the weather a lot faster if you'd both stop...um...helping me.''

There was another moment's silence, and then both man and dog backed out. They didn't leave her, though. She scrambled into shoes, rolled her pillow in the sleeping bag and jacket flapping, poked her head out of the tent. They were both standing there, drenched in the rain, Jezebel's lolling pink tongue the only sign of color in the dark night.

"You didn't have to wait.''

"No? For all I knew you were gonna go back to dreaming about movies.'' A ripple of thunder, low and ear popping, made him grab the sleeping bag and hook an arm around her shoulder at the same time. "Let's go.''

They raced for the front door and pelted inside, gasping and wet. Confusion reigned as they all crowded into the same space. Seth dropped her bag and latched the door; both of them yelped a protest when Jezebel enthusiastically shook all over, spraying raindrops everywhere. Samantha was laughing and she knew she heard Seth chuckling as well.

There was just an instant, when he turned to face her. All the noise and confusion seemed to stop in the spin of a second. Samantha's mouth was still split in a grin—she knew how she looked, dressed in a Cowboys sleep shirt, tennies and jacket, with wet hair dripping down her back in strings. Who cared? They were all safe and out of the storm. And judging from the glint of irrepressible laughter in his eyes, Seth had already found *some* humor in saving a groggy damsel in distress.

He didn't laugh at the look of her, though. In fact, he seemed to freeze, as if he suddenly realized they were standing a hairbreadth from each other. His shoulders locked dead still. Under the artificial hall light, his skin looked oddly flushed, and his gaze riveted on her face with such sharp intensity that she couldn't breathe...and didn't want to. His eyes were luminous, a deeper blue than a midnight sky. She saw hunger in his eyes, a man's hunger and a man's pure, raw sexual awareness. Samantha could have sworn he thought of her as a pesky overfriendly stranger, not that he'd even noticed her as a woman.

He'd noticed. A strange primitive shiver chased up her spine. Fear wasn't the cause. At least, not exactly. The emotional charge between them was rare, unexpected, like the excitement and stomach-dropping thrill of a roller coaster ride. She'd known men. Hundreds. Heck, she'd been playing doctor at a precocious five, but Seth was different than any man she'd known and her racing, thrumming pulse seemed to know it.

He surely felt the same charge—the look in his eyes was telling enough—but his response was quite different. Confronted with an impromptu audit by the

IRS, a man couldn't look more nervous. "I . . . um . . . guess we'd better get you settled upstairs."

"Sure," she agreed.

"Unless you want something to drink? I picked up a few groceries this afternoon. If you need something, the kitchen's—"

"No, that's okay. I'm fine," she said cheerfully. "Just more than grateful for the hospitality. The storm sounds like it's getting worse, doesn't it?"

She kept up the natural chitchat as they mounted the stairs, but it didn't seem to help. He walked as if there were a spike up his spine. To a point she understood. They were strangers. About to spend the night together. That sneaky sizzle of sexual chemistry only complicated a situation that was inherently uncomfortable to begin with, but heavens, this was the '90s. She wasn't about to have an attack of the vapors at the idea of spending a night under his roof. He'd been kind enough to offer her shelter from the storm, nothing else implied. It just wasn't a big deal.

Apparently it was to him. At the top of the stairs, he first pointed out the bathroom, then the master bedroom where he'd been sleeping. Then, rather obviously, he led her to the far, far end of the long, long hall to the farthest bedroom from his.

He flicked on the overhead light. At a glance, she saw the room was tiny, with the charm of a cushion-covered window seat and a brass bed. Three walls were a faded French blue, and the fourth paneled with inset bookcases.

"Sorry. It's just a bare mattress. None of the bedrooms were made up—"

"It doesn't matter. I have my sleeping bag and pillow. This is just terrific. Thanks."

"Are you going to be warm enough?"

"Fine." The way he kept looking at her, she was probably going to toast from the toenails up. He dropped his eyes, fast, and when he carted her sleeping bag to the bed, he made a point of keeping a full foot of distance between them. Samantha suspected he wanted her to feel safe from any murder, rape, or mayhem at his hands, but truthfully, fear of any of those things had never crossed her mind. Not with him.

He ducked his head around the door. "I'm pretty sure there's a lock. All the other doors had keys right in them. Yeah, here—"

"Seth." When he raised his head, she said gently, "I'm not worried about locking the door."

He frowned. "No?"

"No." It was that frown that triggered the irresistible impulse. She'd simply seen that wary frown directed at her once too often. Lord, she thought, some woman must have burned him good. One of them was worried about locked doors, but it certainly wasn't her.

Maybe the devil made her do it, but she crossed the room in three quick steps and rose on tiptoe. He didn't budge, but he sucked in an uneasy breath when her hands slid around his shoulders. Softly, swiftly, she bussed his rain-cooled cheek. And then promptly rocked back on her heels. "Honest to Pete, you can stop worrying. I'm not going to sneak in your room and seduce you in the middle of the night. Not that the idea isn't tempting—you're the sexiest man I've met in a decade—but I'm simply beat. Thanks for everything, Seth. You've been terrifically kind. Good night."

She closed the door, gently, on the frozen, startled look on his face.

And then let out a breath in a whoosh of a sigh that startled her. Kissing him had just been a mischievous impulse. And all she'd done was kiss his cheek, for heaven's sake.

Yet her heart was suddenly beating, beating, beating as if she'd just finished a lap at the Derby. She hadn't noticed until that moment that he'd only yanked on a jacket over his bare chest. His skin was bronze, covered with a thatch of wiry, springy hair. Under the harsh light, his wet hair had been glistening and his face seemed carved in stone and he'd smelled like wind and rain and old leather. Masculine smells, to match all those miles of tough, lean muscle, and Samantha told herself that the combination was enough to make any woman feel some elementally female hormones.

Yet it wasn't hormones, but the look in his eyes that lingered in her mind. His whole body had been cooled down from that foray in the rain, except for his eyes. When she'd leaned up, when she'd so sparely, barely, kissed his cheek, there'd been heat in his eyes, the blue flame of emotion, a glimpse of the real man underneath all the layers of control.

Samantha feathered a hand through her damp hair, unsure why she suddenly felt so shaky. Fear had never been in her vocabulary. Not around men. Any heart that had been used and abused learned to protect itself, and she could handle most men blindfolded with both hands tied behind her back. Seth didn't need "handling." He was just a nice guy. They were two ships passing in the night. He'd been nothing but kind to her—way beyond the call of duty for a stranger—and she deserved three strokes of the guilt lash for teasing him.

Her dad claimed she was born with a streak of mischief. It was true. Her whole life, Samantha had been trying to subdue the devil in her character. Nothing seemed to do any good. Tomorrow, she decided firmly, she'd make it up to him. She'd be polite and serious and an absolute angel of proper behavior.

After unrolling her sleeping bag, she fluffed the pillow, switched off the overhead light and climbed in. It took a moment for her to find a comfortable position. Her feet had to be free—she could never sleep with the sleeping bag zipped—and the old mattress had lumps and bulges that her body had to adjust to. She closed her eyes, and tried to empty her mind of everything but ghosts.

That was, after all, what she was here for. Ghosts. She didn't want to experience a hoard. One would do. Of all the research she'd done, this house had the most history of hauntings and ghost sightings of any along the Maine coast. The original owner, way back in the 1700s, had been a scoundrel of a pirate named Jock. He was the guy who was supposed to haunt the place.

An hour passed. She wasn't even close to sleeping, but her imagination was obligingly working overtime. The storm had moved in full throttle. The old house was full of ghastly creaks and ghostly groans. Wind hissed through the cracks. Rain pounded on the windows; shadows danced on the walls.

The longer she stared at the blue-paneled wall, the more she was positive it moved. Actually moved. As if there were a door-size opening in the wall. For a moment, she actually sensed the presence of someone else in the room. A man. Whose eyes raked the length of her with libidinous interest.

Lord, she thought, imagination was a wonderful thing—and certainly an entertaining cure for insomnia. She yawned sleepily, and turned on her side.

That was when she saw—she *knew* she saw—the doorknob turn. Her heart leapt into her throat. She wasn't exactly afraid. Samantha could let out a bloodcurdling scream that could wake the dead in three counties, if she had to. She could surely wake Seth if there was an intruder. It was just, perhaps, that she was a teensy bit more susceptible to believing in the boogey man than she'd thought.

The door edged open, groaning on rusty hinges. A big black shadow—surely as big as a bear—took a loping gallop and landed with a whomp on the bed. The scream died in her throat. She even let out a weak laugh. "So you can open doors, can you, Jezzie?" she whispered. "Darn it, you scared me half to death. Did he kick you out of bed, poor baby? That's okay. You can stay right here."

The dog was dry, thank heavens, but she certainly crowded the narrow space of the twin bed. Samantha didn't care. She turned on her side, and noted—with no surprise—that the blue-paneled wall was just a wall. No openings. No strange shadows.

She snuggled down and immediately closed her eyes.

Seth couldn't sleep. He'd tried deep-knee bends, tried counting sheep, and at the moment he was trying forty push-ups on the plush Persian rug in his bedroom. It was three in the morning. Something had to wear him out enough to sleep.

It was her—Samantha Adams—who'd rattled him. More specifically, it was her kiss that had rattled him. Sure, it had been just a peck, but for all she knew he was an escaped serial killer on the lam. No woman with a brain went around kissing strange men. She probably thought she was being funny, making that comment about his not needing to worry she was going to seduce him in the middle of the night. Real funny. Real cute.

Legs straight, arms flexed, he touched his chin to the dusty carpet again. It was damn embarrassing that she'd read him so easily. Hell, he'd never been one of those guys with a massive masculine ego, never thought he was so irresistible that any woman would just outright come on to him. But damn. He wasn't sure of her. She radiated more sexual chemistry than any ten women. She struck him as totally unpredictable, a wild card. A woman who wouldn't think twice before giving in to an impulse.

She'd be in for a hell of a shock if she tried taking out an impulse—at least any sexual impulse—on him.

Shoulders sheened and damp, chest heaving, Seth quit the push-ups and rolled over on his back. Probably inevitably, his unexpected houseguest made him think of Gail. When his mind was on sex, he *always* thought of Gail.

They'd been engaged. He'd known her for more than a year, met her on a crazy spring day. She'd had a flat tire en route to a wedding, and he'd stopped to help her. He'd been in jeans and work clothes; she'd been decked out in formal, lacy wedding gear, a blue dress, the same color as her eyes. She was Ms. Bouncing Energy, always flying this way and that, couldn't relax to save her life. An acrobat in bed. She'd taught him a thing or two, and there was *nothing* she wasn't interested in trying.

Maybe he hadn't tried hard enough. Maybe he should have picked up the obvious clue when she'd been so stubborn about keeping her apartment until after the wedding. He wasn't likely to forget the afternoon he'd popped in on her unexpectedly—wanting to surprise her; it was rare he could steal a couple hours off—and found her in bed with someone else. The guy was muscle bound. Gail always did like muscles. And she'd worked up those guy's muscles to a healthy sweat.

It killed him. Seth had told himself a million times that the rip and tear should have healed by now. In the sense that he was over Gail, it had. He had some archaic values about fidelity. Gail's bed hopping had permanently erased her from his map. But months ago, he'd found someone else—hardly a kindred spirit but someone to share a night with. He'd flopped like a pancake. God knew his deprived hormones had been geared up. God knew the lady had been willing. But he'd started worrying about pleasing her, couldn't shake the lead weight of awareness that he'd clearly and obviously failed to sexually satisfy Gail, and damned if he hadn't wilted like a faded rose.

Wilt.

Him.

The humiliation had hit him with the impact of a two-ton megabomb. Maybe there was nothing special about him, maybe there was nothing there to make him rise above the label of "ordinary guy," but one thing he'd always been sure of was sex. He'd never taken a woman to bed where he didn't care about her feelings and needs. To his knowledge, he'd always been a good lover. Aw, hell. There was a time he thought he was a *great* lover. His one intensely private claim to fame.

That one had sure been blown out of the water. Seth didn't plan on a permanent celibate life-style. It was just for now. Right now, his interest in getting naked with a woman, on a scale of one to ten, was a negative five thousand. Speaking conservatively. He'd rather chew rats than risk another experience with humiliation and failure.

With an exasperated sigh, Seth lurched to his feet. It wasn't as if he hadn't covered this ground in his mind before, and he'd *never* sleep if he started dwelling on it. Absently he glanced around. "Jezzie? Jezebel?"

The last he noticed, the pup had been lying at the foot of his bed. She was gone now. And damn, the bedroom door was open.

Without turning on a light, he padded barefoot into the hall, calling to her in a low whisper. He stopped dead when he realized the door to the blue bedroom was cracked open. It was Samantha Adams that had aroused all those anxiety-ridden memories, and the one thing he did *not* want to do was go anywhere near her bedroom.

He hesitated. He could hear snoring coming from that open door. Big, heavy, husky snores. It was possible, of course, that Samantha was a snorer. But fairly unlikely that she'd suddenly developed the volume and voice of an overweight trucker.

Trying to be as quiet as a mouse, he poked his head in. The storm had long ceased, and moonlight streamed on the huge black shadow on her bed. Jezzie promptly woke, lifted her head and thumped her tail louder than the thwack of a hammer.

"Shhhh!" He didn't notice that Samantha's legs were uncovered, bared to the top of her hips, slim and white. He didn't notice the dark hair streaming like sensual black ribbons against her creamy throat. He didn't notice that she'd thrown off the sleeping bag cover completely, and the V-neck of her sleep shirt dipped alluringly over the crest of one breast.

Seth was an extremely smart man. Too smart to notice things he shouldn't. Even looking at Samantha Adams was a reminder of his worst nightmare. Damned if he was going to let himself be tempted.

He pantomimed to the dog to *get down* and *come,* making wild hand gestures in the dark. Jezzie showed no inclination to obey, although her tail whacked the mattress with increasing enthusiasm.

"It's okay, Seth," Samantha murmured sleepily. "She can stay with me. I think she's still afraid of the ghost. We're kind of protecting each other."

He'd have flushed from mortification if she'd seen his pantomining antics, but as far as he could tell, she hadn't. She never opened her eyes. That sleepy voice might have come straight from a man's dream. And damned if she didn't spout sheer nonsense about ghosts even when she was sound asleep.

He padded back to his bedroom, mentally lecturing himself for making mountains out of molehills. So she had the kind of looks to make his hormones feel frisky and reckless. So he couldn't stop worrying that a woman that batty and impractical wasn't safe running loose around the country. So what?

He had a ton of work to do tomorrow. If she wanted to look around for *ghosts* for a few hours, she wasn't likely to be in his way. There was no possible harm. No danger. She was such a kook that she hardly represented a serious temptation.

Nothing, Seth promised himself, could possibly happen between them that he needed to worry about.

Four

———

Seth drummed his fingers on the kitchen counter. Maybe she'd spent the night, but this hardly qualified as a typical morning after. What was a guy supposed to do under these circumstances? Offer breakfast as if she were an invited guest? Assume she already had food packed somewhere in that soggy tent?

The last of the pancakes were sizzling around the edges. After flipping them with the spatula, he peered into the oven where he was keeping the first batches warm. He seemed to have made a hundred. Enough to cover all bases. Assuming she ever woke up. His stomach was grumbling impatiently—it was already past ten. The sun was long up. He had mountains of work to do. Jezebel had already been taken on a long walk along the ocean; she'd come home to level two bowls of breakfast and was now trying to snooze on his feet, making cooking on the grill a near life-threatening experience.

"Morning, Seth."

He couldn't spin around with one hundred and fifty pounds on his feet, but he twisted fast. "Morning." Right off she reminded him of how hungry he was, but darned if he could keep his mind on food. He'd dragged her inside last night before giving her a chance to grab any spare clothes, so it wasn't her fault that she was still wearing the Cowboys sleep shirt and hell, modesty was no issue. Its size had to be an extra large men's; it fell to her knees and fit like an oversize tent. Sort of. The fabric intimately draped some distinctive feminine bumps and slopes; she was barefoot, and her dark eyes had the sleepy sensuality of a hedonistic lover. "I was beginning to wonder if you were ever going to wake up."

"Actually I've been up for a while. I've just been meditating."

"Ah. Meditating." Seth cleared his throat. "Do you want some breakfast? Pancakes?"

"Sure, if you have enough."

He had enough, but it was tough getting anything on the table. Jezzie thwacked her tail in enthusiastic greeting, making Samantha promptly crouch down to pet her. That made two of them to step over. "Is this the lover who kept me so warm last night? Is it? Why, you're just a big old snuggly bear, aren't you, baby?" She lifted her head. "What can I do to help?"

Several answers shot through his mind. Not wear V-necked sleep shirts that showed off the shadow of her breasts. Shave her head, so all that satiny dark hair would quit catching the light. Not look at him with those lethally pretty eyes. "Not a thing. Except come to the table."

Both of them obeyed that call to arms, but Seth made Jezzie lie back down again. Samantha wasn't shy about heaping her plate or in lavishing praise. "I haven't had pancakes in a blue moon. These are wonderful."

"A guy alone has to learn to cook. Although breakfast's my best shot. Can't seem to work all day without something serious in my stomach to start with." With some amazement, he watched her keeping up with him. Gail used to peck like a bird, and pepper the conversation every meal with talk about diets.

Their hands collided when they both reached for the syrup. Seth dropped his hand quickly. Not that he wanted to avoid even a chance accidental physical contact between them, but he had a feeling it wasn't wise to get between that woman and her food.

"Am I going to bother you if I stick around?"

"I already told you it'd be okay. I have stuff to do, but you can look for...um...ghosts all you want." He couldn't help but add dryly, "I don't expect it'll take you very long."

"Oh, I don't know. This house has the most potential for atmosphere I've found so far. Last night, I could have sworn I actually felt another presence in the bedroom."

"Did you? Sounds like a real thrill."

She had to catch the open skepticism in his tone, because her eyes met his with a mischievous glint of humor. As serious as a judge, though, she trilled on. "There's supposed to be a pirate haunting this house. A guy named Jock. I've found mentions of him all over the place . . . 1860. A lady's diary. Druscilla Ransome. Her father was one of the owners of the house. Anyway, her dad was trying to keep her from seeing this boy she loved, even went so far as to lock her in her bedroom—the green one upstairs. She wrote in her diary that this Jock got her out, unlocked the window, so her lover could get to her. They escaped and eloped.''

"Is that conclusive evidence of ghosts or what. Do you want some more pancakes?''

"Maybe a few." Her eyes were outright dancing now. "There was another record. I found some letters between two women, really old letters, dated in the 1820s. This one lady, Martha, described the same pirate ghost. Same name of Jock. She claimed he locked this gentleman in the house with her, fixed it so they couldn't unlatch a single door or window. They ended up together all night, but naturally, in those times, her reputation was ruined. All's well that ends well—they ended up married. Happily married. Martha gave all the credit to the ghost.''

Seth swallowed quickly. "Golly. Two stories about the same ghost. I can hardly contain my excitement, but I'm gonna try. You want some coffee?''

She shook her head on a bubble of laughter. "No, thanks. I'm fine.''

It was the only thing she'd turned down yet. Seth gave up all pretense of eating and cupped his chin in his palm to watch her. Her manners were impeccable, no spills, no crumbs. But the pancakes were disappearing at the speed of light. If she made love with that kind of voracious, uninhibited appetite, her lover would have a heart attack from exhaustion before he got to second base. But Lord, would he die happy.

Seth banished that dangerous train of thought before it could go any further. "Hasn't anyone ever fed you before?"

"Pardon?"

He motioned to the nearly empty platter. "Where on earth are you putting it?"

"My dad used to say I had hollow legs." With a cheeky grin, she lifted one long limb to demonstrate. It didn't look hollow to him. The delicate ankle, the shapely slope of calf, was distinctly feminine flesh and blood, but she tucked the leg back under her before he could be caught looking too hard. Surprising him not at all, she went right back to talking nonsense. "You might not be too quick to believe in ghosts, but Jezebel's acted spooked a couple of times, haven't you noticed? I think *she* believes me."

"You only met Jezzie yesterday, or you'd already know that she spooks if a mouse runs across the floor. And she slept with you last night, didn't she? She obviously got over being afraid."

"Or maybe the ghost made friends with her."

Seth rolled his eyes. "Why am I getting the bad, bad feeling that you still believe in fairy tales?"

"Not fairy tales. Too many of those Prince Charmings had the nasty habit of taking over their princesses' lives, but I confess to having a soft spot for old romantic movies."

He remembered. Trying to wake her last night, the lightning storm threatening them both with imminent electrocution, she'd murmured something inane about a Cary Grant film. Her impractical romantic nature was obvious. Maybe there was something about her that made his pulse thump Me Tarzan, You Jane, but Seth figured he'd be perfectly safe as long as he remembered that she was *Casablanca* and he was strictly *Die Hard.*

"Guess I'm not going to convince you about the ghost, hmm?" Finally she set down her fork with a throaty sigh of satisfaction. She should be sighing, Seth thought. She'd leveled a marine sergeant's quota of food.

They both lurched up to clear the dishes at the same time. Jezzie, mistakenly hoping for leftovers and knowing Seth wasn't likely to sucker in, tangoed and tangled around Samantha's legs. "How on earth did you happen to name her Jezebel?" she asked with a laugh.

"The obvious reason. Even as a pup, it seemed to fit her personality. As you can see, she doesn't put a lot of stock in faithfulness. Hell, she'd go off with the dog catcher if he talked to her nice."

He'd meant her to smile again. So far she'd grinned at all of his straight lines, and knowing she had a sense of humor had made the breakfast conversation come oddly natural and easy. Just then, though, the smile faded from her soft red mouth. She just looked at him, suddenly, quietly, as if clues to a puzzle were clicking into place and she guessed he'd known a woman who fit that epitaph of Jezebel.

"Look, I don't care if you look around," he said swiftly, "but I honestly don't have time to play host. For starters I need to hit a hardware store, so I'm not even going to be around here—"

"It's okay," she said gently.

He had the confounded sensation she was trying to reassure him about something different than his bad manners at leaving her alone. Whatever. It didn't work. Nightmares had plagued his sleep the night before...raw, naked fantasies of her wound around his body tighter than instant glue...and yeah, his failing her when it counted. The dreams were stupid, and he'd wakened feeling edgy and angry with himself. Right then he'd made up his mind that if she wanted to stick around, she could. What if she tried that ghost baloney on somebody else? Some guy who'd take one look at those eyes and long legs and decide to act out his own version of those instant-glue fantasies? At least she was safe with him. *That,* Seth could guarantee with his heart, soul and life savings.

Impatiently he jammed a wallet into his jeans back pocket and grabbed his truck keys. She was safe. He was safe. Everybody was safe, but there wasn't a woman who'd made him this nervous since he was a libidinous teenager. He wanted to get out of there. Quickly. And he did.

Samantha had brought a satchel full of research. She spent several hours comparing references in notes and letters to the actual rooms in the house, but it was tough to keep her mind on ghosts with all the pounding and strange noises going on. Seth had closed the door to the kitchen when he returned home from the hardware store. She had no idea what he was doing in there, but my midafternoon, she headed downstairs, stepped over a napping Jezzie in the hallway and aimed for the kitchen door.

She wasn't nosy. Just curious. Any woman would understand the difference, Samantha assured herself, and she opened the door to steal a peek.

One short peek, unfortunately, led to a long, astonished stare. Only hours before, the kitchen had been pristine clean and neat. Now it was in total shambles.

Every single cupboard door and drawer hung open. Tarps covered the redbrick floor. The back door and windows were cranked open, apparently to dissipate the acrid, stinky smell of the paint stripper he was using. The fresh air helped, but the weird smell still pervaded everything. A third of the cupboards were no longer white, but naked wood. Pecan, she guessed. Another third were covered with a gunk that looked like thick bubbling goo, reminding Samantha of the blob stuff in horror movies.

"Can I help?" she asked from the doorway.

Seth wheeled around on his haunches, clearly not expecting to see her. He'd worked up a sweat, thrown his shirt somewhere, and was only wearing thick work gloves, boots and jeans. His bare shoulders glowed with a pagan sheen under the bright kitchen light, and his chin and chest had dirt smudges.

Just the look of him was enough to make her pulse thud. She was getting used to it—the pulse thud, the cluster of hormones pooling low in her stomach, the sudden staccato beat of her heart. It happened whenever she was near him. The gaze he swiveled toward her was buckshot with wintery wariness...but she was getting used to that, too.

She'd thought all day about the reason that he'd named his dog Jezebel. It took no psychic perception to guess that Seth had a cheating lover in his past. However badly the woman had hurt him, though, she thankfully hadn't squelched his natural sense of humor. Samantha caught the edge of an unwilling grin. Her offer to help had divertingly aroused his funny bone.

"You gotta be kidding," he said wryly.

"I'm not. Can't I help?"

"No, of course not." His gaze slewed down her body like a wash of warm rain. "You'd wreck your hands. You'd ruin your clothes. Trust me, this isn't the kind of mess you want to be anywhere around."

Her ocher shirt and khaki shorts probably wouldn't survive any serious work, but she spotted a rumpled, paint-spattered coverall on a chair. He'd probably been too hot to wear it. "I could use that. There has to be something I could do. It sure looks like you have your hands full."

"It'll get done. It isn't hard work, just messy and slow. Thanks for the offer, but it really isn't necessary."

He didn't outright say "skedaddle," but Samantha picked up the subtle suggestion in his tone. Honestly. Some men just seemed to be born with a bullheaded stubborn streak. Maybe some Jezebel in his life had made him feel real, real wary around the female of the species, but for heaven's sakes. She was hardly threatening to throw him on the floor and have her wicked way with him. She was just offering to help. Anyone with a brain could see that he was neck deep in a mess that could clearly be tackled faster with two sets of hands.

"Just tell me what you're doing," she coaxed. "I mean . . . how does that stuff work?"

Apparently he didn't mind answering her questions, as long as he could work at the same time. He explained the process of stripping—paint the stuff on, wait until it bubbled, then stroke it off with a putty knife—while she watched the process. His back was already turned to her. He wasn't being rude. Obviously when the yucky stuff bubbled, it had to be handled right then.

Still watching, Samantha quickly pulled her hair back in a ponytail. Just as quickly, she climbed into the pair of coveralls. Cuffed four times at the ankles, and just as many times at the wrists, the outfit still swam on her. She found a second pair of work gloves—actually two pairs—in a box with all his tools on the floor. They didn't fit, either. My Lord, the man had hands bigger than boulders.

Seth didn't look around until he heard her rummaging through his toolbox for another paintbrush. Then his jaw seemed to drop about an inch and a half.

"Don't you dare give me a hard time," she warned him. "I've leveled bigger men than you who tried to argue with me, and I watched everything you're doing. It's just like you said—messy and slow work—but nothing you couldn't teach a rookie to do. A house has a way of turning into a disaster when the kitchen's torn up. The faster you get this done, the better. You offered me hospitality last night and the least—the very least—you can do is let me pay you back by helping. Otherwise, I'll just feel bad. Extremely bad. Do you want that on your conscience? Do you?"

It was probably the threat of her leveling him that brought him around. Not that he looked terrified, but he had a heck of a time holding back a slow, dry grin. He only tried one last protest. "I thought you were supposed to be real busy, searching for ghosts. What happened, did you give up?"

"Heavens, no. It just wasn't the right afternoon to pick up psychic vibrations." She hunched down next to him, thinking that she was never going to be able to control the devil in her character when it brought such results. How could she resist teasing him? His expression so clearly gave away what he thought of anything remotely connected to "psychic vibrations." "I tried a little crystal channeling," she said gravely. "Even consulted the *I Ching*. Apparently I just need to wait until tomorrow."

"You're planning on still being here tomorrow?"

She wasn't sure if the sudden alarm in his expression was caused by the idea of her sticking around, or the imminent threat she posed with a putty knife in her hand. "I've barely started my research. But I certainly won't stay if I'm in your way. If you're afraid I was going to impose on you in the house again—it's been sunshiny all day, I can easily camp in my tent."

"The ground's as wet as a marsh. You'll catch pneumonia sleeping outside—aw, hell." The question of where she was sleeping or staying was abruptly tabled. "Cripes, you've already got the stuff all over you."

Samantha noticed. The paint stripper was truly the ickiest substance she'd ever come across, and though she wasn't inclined to admit it to Seth, physical labor was not exactly her forte. By six o'clock, her neck ached, her wrists hurt and more muscles were creaking and groaning than she'd ever known she had.

It was done, though. She had no idea what he was going to do with all that bare wood, but at least the paint was all stripped. She peeled off the coveralls and stretched like a cream-sated cat. Tiredness didn't matter; she felt buoyantly high on pure satisfaction. They'd accomplished an enormous amount.

"But you're not going to be able to cook in here," she mused.

"Not for a couple of days," Seth agreed. He'd gotten used to her starting a dialogue midthought.

"We could drag some wood near the beach. Grill some steaks or burgers over a fire," she suggested.

When he hesitated, Samantha figured he just wasn't sure of that "we." As far as she could tell, he was still confused about how they'd managed to work side-by-side all afternoon—much less have a terrific good time doing it.

"Okay, Connor. Let's have this out." Samantha pushed up her sleeves. "Do you want me out of your hair?"

"I never said that."

"You don't have to be kind. It's your house. I'm the interloper. I can easily understand if you don't want me—" A poor choice of words, she realized instantly, because Seth's seventeen-inch neck flushed red.

"I didn't say that, either."

It was her turn to hesitate. She couldn't pretend being unaware that she made him uncomfortable. And she could easily solve that problem lickety-split—by taking off. Although she was honestly fascinated with the ghost lore associated with the Connor house, Maine was peppered with colorful history. She could go somewhere else. If she was truthful—with herself—ghost lore was the last thing on her mind when she was with Seth.

Lord. She'd only known him for a few concentrated hours. Hardly long enough to feel a kismet and kindred spirit draw. Maybe a battered heart recognized another battered heart? She'd never experienced a faithless lover, but she was a world-class pro at attracting men who wanted to use her. Although he couldn't know it, she'd learned to be wary of trust, too. She liked Seth's sense of humor; she liked his straightforward style and his honest eyes, and more than anything—for the first time in an eon—she'd found a man who truly wanted nothing from her. She wanted to stay.

But not if her being around was going to cause him grief. She sensed a painful loneliness in Seth, but she'd have to be blind and batty not to recognize how hard he worked to avoid even the most accidental touch between them. He'd been hurt. She didn't want to add to that, and the only safe choice she could possibly make was to simply leave.

So she would, she decided, and opened her mouth to say just that . . . when his stomach suddenly grumbled. Loudly. His eyes rolled in embarrassment. She had to chuckle.

"I think we'd better feed you quick before you faint from hunger," she teased him. Her conscience promptly let out a squawk. She added smoothly, "I'll just stay for dinner, if that's all right with you, but after that I'll be on my way."

When he made no protest, she knew she'd made the right decision. Unfortunately time seemed to steal away from both of them. Tools and paintbrushes needed cleaning up, and after that, they both wanted to shower and change clothes. Seth had purchased steaks on his grocery trip the day before; Samantha fetched baking potatoes from her stock of food and gathered silverware and paper plates.

More than an hour passed before they headed outside. By then, the sun had dropped. A winsome spring breeze wafted off the ocean. The sky had darkened to a deep royal blue, shot with streaks of violets and soft scarlets. It was high tide, the waves no stronger than frothing bubbles that ebbed and flowed on the rocks.

Seth built the fire in the lee of a bouldered cove. Constructing the fire took both time and a lot of humorous swearing, because Jezebel kept taking off with his kindling. By the time the blaze lit up the sky with sparks, Samantha had a hoard of sticks at her feet— Jezzie's gift of stolen loot.

The steaks were juicy and hot and they both devoured them like ravenous wolves. Seth kept forking more food onto her plate, making deadpan comments about bottomless wells, black holes and never meeting a woman before who could outeat his dog. She told him she'd grown up with two older sisters— meaning that his teasing was a waste of breath; she'd already been insulted by *real* pros. Eventually stuffed, though, she had to plead mercy.

"You mean you're finally full? Hell, Jezzie, did you hear that? I think we're witnessing a record event."

She tossed a wadded-up napkin in retaliation for his totally faked look of awe, but he just caught it with a grin. The night had turned a pitchy, witchy black by then. When Seth settled back against a rock, she caught a look at his face by firelight. Shadows played on the crinkled lines around his eyes, the strong bones and natural curve of his mouth.

Sleepy butterflies fluttered in her stomach. It was the first time she'd seen Seth relax—at least around her. He was beat, so was she, but it was so easy to see that this was what he loved. Simple things. The lull of ocean surf, the smell of woodsmoke, the crackle and hiss of a dying fire, the savoring of a velvet peaceful night. When had she ever found a man who naturally and honestly enjoyed the same things she did?

She had to leave, she reminded herself, but the temptation to linger a little longer was impossible to resist. Lazily she leaned back against a rock, rolling her shoulders to chase out the kinks.

"You're sore, aren't you?"

"A little," she admitted.

"I shouldn't have let you work so long. You can't be used to physical labor like that."

"You didn't ask me. I volunteered, remember?" She shot him a grin. "But you couldn't be more right. It's been a hundred years since I did any honest physical work. Honest to Pete, I loved every minute of it. In my family, it just wasn't allowed."

"Not allowed?"

She leaned her head back and half closed her eyes. "Where I grew up, if anything needed fixing in the house, we hired it done. No one had time. My mom's an attorney, seriously involved in politics around Phillie. My father's in business. Both of them come from landed money, but they still work seventy-hour weeks. My sisters—Jennifer and Trish—both work just as hard. Picking up a paintbrush would have been frowned on...so would cooking over a fire, like this...and heaven knows, no one would dare take time to smell the roses. If you're an Adams, all your time is supposed to be committed to worthy, responsible causes."

Seth didn't respond, but she could feel his eyes on her face. He was listening. The fire was toasting her toes; the dinner had made her feel sleepy and warm, and the combination seemed to disastrously loosen her tongue.

"Afraid I was always the black sheepess in the family. The lazy mongrel. The rebel with absolutely no cause. Last fall, though, I was real close to suckering in." She made a vague gesture with her hand. "There was a man in the wings. The Right Kind of Man. The whole family decided that Joe was perfect for me. My dad wanted to give us a two-story colonial house for a wedding present. I think that was the last straw."

"You were engaged to this guy?" Seth asked sharply.

"Not engaged. But Joe was definitely hinting about rings." She gestured again. "I've seen marriages work. Lots of them. People who build a relationship out of mutual interests and mutual backgrounds. My family was pushing hard, he was pushing even harder—and it wasn't as if I didn't care about him. I did. But I kept having these claustrophobic nightmares about being trapped and closed-in. And I had the nasty intuition that if the pressure kept up, I was going to cave in and say yes. So I hit the road."

"You left this...Joe...hanging?"

"No. I cut it off with him. Which made my family really furious with me." Samantha sighed. "They think it's past time I settled down, picked up the Adams banner of responsibility and behaved myself."

"I can't imagine why they'd want their daughter settled in a secure relationship instead of wandering across the country and sleeping in pup tents," Seth murmured dryly.

"Hey. *Et tu, brute?*"

"The guy didn't sound so bad."

"He wasn't. But there was a teensy bug in the soup I didn't mention." She hesitated. "Joe liked the idea of my father buying us a house. He liked the idea even more of my mom using her influence to get him into a prestigious law firm. I'm not blaming Joe for being ambitious—but it's happened before. About a dozen times. Men who assumed that a ring on my finger came with package benefits, because I was an Adams. I just needed to get away and be alone for a while. Does that sound so terrible?''

Seth said quietly, ''No.''

Samantha couldn't see his expression. He chose that moment to lean forward to throw a stick for Jezzie, who promptly bounded into the surf to fetch it. She suddenly felt itchy and unsettled. It had been an impulse to share her background with him, a chance to communicate that she wasn't remotely like his Jezebel. But possibly steering anywhere near serious subjects was a mistake. She wanted to kick herself— they'd been doing fine with lightweight conversation and breezy teasing.

''At the end of six months... are you planning on going back home?'' he asked her.

This time she was careful to keep her tone airy and light. ''Sure. No matter what, they're my family and I love them. And I've got an apartment in Phillie that's costing me a ridiculous amount of rent if I'm not even there to enjoy it. But that six months was never set in granite. I'm not about to go home...'' She raised a mischievous eyebrow. ''Until I've found some ghosts.''

Dark humor glinted in his eyes, exactly what she'd hoped for. ''You believe in ghosts,'' he said dryly, ''about as much as I do. I don't think you buy into that I-Ching or crystal channeling nonsense, either. In fact, I keep getting the feeling that the whole irresponsible 'black sheepess' image is a hoax, Ms. Adams.''

''Hey. I've gone to all this trouble, giving you my spoiled-little-rich-girl story, trying to impress you with how lazy and rootless and uncommitted I am. Haven't you listened to a word?"

"Yeah, I listened. I listened about the ghosts, too. Come on. Admit it. You believe you're gonna connect with some psychic spirit like you'd buy swamp land in Arizona."

"My heavens," she murmured suddenly.

"My heavens what?"

"Look." She looked to her feet and motioned toward the house. Fog was starting to form down the coastline, wisping around the abandoned white lighthouse and through the distant trees. They'd left no lights on. Clouds skuttled across the moon, adding to the silky darkness, but light still reflected off the black windows. On a third floor window, a curtain moved. Pulled back. As if by an unseen hand. "Did you see that?"

Seth frowned. "It's just an illusion. Shadows moving."

Samantha shook her head, her gaze still magneted to the window. "I think it's in the blue bedroom. The one where I slept last night." The curtain pulled back farther. Something moved behind it. The distance had to be three hundred yards, but she could swear she saw a man's face. "I told you there were ghosts, didn't I? I told you about Jock. Now do you believe me?"

Five

Seth scowled up at the window. There was nothing
there. Nothing. For a brief two seconds, it *looked* as
if a man's face had been pressed against the second-
story window. Hell, the house was a few hundred
yards away, and shadows flickered everywhere on a
foggy night like this. The reflection had clearly been
an illusion. Certainly not a *ghost*.

Only Samantha Adams would come to such a
cockamamy conclusion.

The sound of a high-pitched feminine chortle made
him whip his head around. Jezebel had gotten it into
her head that Samantha wanted her face washed.
Giggling and gasping, Samantha twisted to her feet
and took off down the beach with the dog chasing at
her heels.

Seth dragged a hand through his hair. If that wasn't
just like her. Scare a man half to death—send shivers

down his spine, for cripes sake—and then blithely forget the whole thing. Hunkering down, he started scooping dirt onto the fire. The paper plates and cups were already burned. Beyond taking in the silverware and putting out the fire, there wasn't any cleanup from dinner to be done.

Two galloping banshees streaked past him. The one in the rag-tail sweatshirt and flapping jacket looked about thirteen, as wild as an uninhibited teenager, her laughter ringing through the night with abandon.

"Jezzie, play gentle," Seth called out, then wondered why he'd bothered wasting his breath. Neither of them listened. He had as much control over those two as he did over White House politics.

Absently he massaged the throbbing in his temples. A tension headache, he thought. He wasn't sure. He'd never been prone to any kind of headache until thirty hours ago when Samantha had walked into his life.

Even before she'd admitted to a blueblood, come-from-money background, he'd known they were Mutt and Jeff. She was as exotic as a bird of paradise. He was as down-home ordinary as meat loaf. She was a cockeyed romantic; he was a practical realist. No sane person had a blast stripping paint—it was a rotten, dirty job—but she had. She did everything with hedonistic, passionate enthusiasm, whether it was working or laughing...or teasing him. Good grief. Her voice even had sleepy, sensual undertones when she talked to the *dog*.

Samantha would be a terrifying handful for any man, Seth thought. Except, of course, for him. He was smart enough to keep a ten-foot-pole physical distance. In good time—his own time, when he got around to feeling ready—he'd take a risk with a woman again. Someone nice, safe, sweet. Not her. Samantha had more natural passion in her fingertips than any woman he'd ever met; it was no surprise when she mentioned the number of guys who'd chased her. And all Ivy League types. Seth wasn't in that competitive league, in bed or out of it, and even thinking about the sexual experience she probably had between the sheets was enough to give him hives.

All he felt for her, Seth told himself judiciously, was a logical, protective case of brotherly-type worry. The damn woman was traipsing around the country. Alone. No sense of caution around strangers, no toughness to her, that sensual nature of hers right out in the open, and a past history—she'd admitted it—of attracting guys who were users. She'd been hurt by that Joe. Seth could understand, better than anyone, the need to hide away and heal after taking a serious heart blow. He knew exactly how vulnerable she felt. By comparison, a baby in a lion's den couldn't be more vulnerable than Samantha. How could he *not* feel as if she needed someone to watch over her?

The banshees cavorted past him again. Samantha was playing hide-the-stick. It was Jezzie's favorite game, but Seth abruptly frowned. "Jezzie. *Jezebel. Not so rough.*"

He figured she'd have the common sense not to roughhouse with a dog who was forty pounds bigger than her.

Apparently not.

When he saw her go down, his boots were already making fast tracks down the rocks and over the lawn. He heard her. She was still giggling. But she was also buried—completely, as far as he could tell—under a smothering blanket of curly black fur. Jezebel didn't have a mean bone in her whole canine body, but the damn doofus was easily heavy enough to crush her fragile ribs.

The two of them were rolling down the slope of the lawn when he caught up with them. "Jezebel. *No.*" He didn't have to scold twice. It was so rare he used that tone of voice that Jezebel knew he meant business. She promptly climbed off her playmate and sat, tail wagging.

Seth only had eyes for the sprawled figure in the glistening-wet grass. The fog rolling in blurred all the edges in the darkness. For that first second, all he could see was her white face and that she wasn't moving. "Damn. Are you okay? It's my fault, because she's used to playing with me. She can't tell the difference when someone's a lot smaller than I am. Double damn. You're covered with..."

She was covered with everything. Bits of wet grass. Dirt. Sand. Her hair was all tangled, her clothes askew. As he pulled her to her feet, he tried to straighten and brush and fix at the same time.

He never planned on kissing her. Never. He didn't even know how it happened. He was worried that she might be hurt; he was trying to brush the twigs out of her hair, trying to see if she was steady on her feet. Yeah, they were standing close, heartbeat close. Yeah, the pad of his thumb brushed her cheek. And yeah, he suddenly saw the luminous glow in her eyes when she lifted her head.

But he never actually saw the earth quit spinning on its axis. He never heard the ocean shut off its surf sounds. He never felt the plain-old-ordinary night turn silky black.

Their lips met. It was all he knew. The texture of her mouth was lush and soft, a cushion under his. She tasted warm, like sunshine. She tasted wild and breathless.

Hesitant, slow, her slim hands slid over the clenched muscles of his shoulders, and then wrapped around his neck. God knew how many men she'd kissed. She knew how, that was for sure. She knew how to kiss so well that a man could go near crazy to woo another one. Fingertips stroked the coarse hair at his nape. Soft fingertips. She leaned into him, the edge of her jacket zipper biting into his chest. He caught glimpses of her white throat in the darkness, bared for his eyes, making his blood rush. Her hair, silky and thick, spilled through his hands. And the whole time her mouth kept moving under his, silver smooth, warm, in a kiss that kept deepening like a dive underwater.

He felt as if he'd been hit with a depth charge. He wasn't sure what had lit her fuse, but it seemed impossibly unlikely that it was him. A sixteen-year-old boy dreamed that a girl would kiss him that way. So did thirty-two-year-old men, but it was just a fantasy, nothing a guy ever expected to come true. No woman chucked all sense and offered her mouth and body with complete abandon, swept away under the potent impact of his virility and masculine chemistry. A guy liked to think it could happen. He liked to think that somewhere, somehow, there was a woman who ignited when he touched her, just when he touched her, as if no other man ever existed for her but him.

Seth would be the first to admit that, in the privacy of their minds, men had some really stupid fantasies.

But damn. That was how she made him feel. Not like she was seducing him, but like the surprise of a kiss had ripped loose her defenses and made her vulnerable, and she liked it, wanted it, wanted *him*. Layers of clothes separated them, but he could feel her breasts, full and straining taut against his chest. His hands scraped down her back. He didn't mean to. His hands were rough, callused, an untenable contrast to her pampered soft skin, and he sure-as-sunshine didn't know her well enough to cup her bottom.

She'd sock him, he thought. And God, he'd deserve it.

But she didn't haul off and hit him. She made a sound, a throaty murmur, as if she liked the feel of his hands on her fanny, liked being pulled rubbing-tight against him. Liquid heat. It seemed to pour off them both, her breath, her delicate feminine scent triggering an arousal harder than stone. His tongue found hers. He took her mouth. Again. Again. A lake of water couldn't quench his thirst, not this sudden desperate thirst he had for her. Her hands tightened in his hair, clenched, holding on as though she'd fall if he dared let her go.

He wasn't about to let her go. He tracked kisses down her long white throat, his stubbled cheek nuzzling against her softer flesh before coming back to her mouth again. She murmured his name as if she was calling him, urgently, as if she'd been lost for a long time and finally found him. He kissed her again, pushing at her jacket and sweatshirt, needing the feel of her bare skin. His hands roamed the feminine hollow of her back, the arch of her spine. A thin strip of bra was in his way. His thumb snapped the catch. Her whole body tightened, keening closer, her mouth melting under his in sweet, naked invitation.

His response was as volatile as mercury. He could have her, he realized. He could take her right here—she wouldn't stop him—and nothing in his life had ever seemed so right. His lungs were starved for a burst of air. He didn't care. He'd never felt this way with another woman, never dreamed he could make a woman as hot and wild as she was, never expected, anywhere, that he would find someone who fit like a glove on his soul. If she was a witch, he wanted the spell. If he was dreaming this, he didn't want to wake up.

From nowhere, something cold and wet nuzzled his hand. A drizzly wet tongue, followed by a distinctly doggy whine. Jezzie. She didn't mind the humans having fun; she just wanted in on the cuddle.

Seth's eyes shot open. Reality returned faster than a slammed door. They were standing in the middle of the yard. The salt air, the misty, foggy shadows, the soaked grass, and yeah, his whining behemoth of a lonesome dog were all real.

So were the warning sirens screaming in his mind. A lump formed in his throat, thicker than glue. He'd never lost his head with a woman, ever, and the one woman he knew—he *knew*—he couldn't touch was her. My God, Gail had been tame compared to the explosive sensuality so natural in Samantha. He'd fail her, sure as hell. He'd proved himself mortifyingly inadequate before, so how could he possibly satisfy a woman so attuned to her senses, so pure vibrantly female, so uninhibited that a chance kiss had ignited a near maelstrom?

Her lashes fluttered up. Her mouth was red, swollen from his kisses, her eyes cloudy and sleepy when she finally focused on him. He clamped his hands on her waist. Tight. Because, dammit, he was afraid she'd fall if he didn't. "I'm sorry."

"Sorry?"

She didn't act as if she recognized the word. She looked at him, her face flushed with radiance even in the shadows, her eyes blind with emotion that she didn't even try to conceal. He was still hotter than a firecracker. His arousal was jammed and cramped in his jeans to the point of pain. If she kept looking at him that way, he was never going to cool down. "Look. I didn't mean anything like that to happen."

"Maybe—" her face tilted to his, her breath still coming out in a whisper of a sigh "—maybe that was why it was so special. Because neither of us meant it to happen."

He dropped his hands—she was finally steady enough—but darned if he knew what he was supposed to do then. He'd feel more comfortable handling lit dynamite. And surely a lot safer. "I'm sorry," he repeated.

"Seth, it's okay. There's nothing to be sorry for." But her soft smile faded as she studied his face. She came awake quickly then, straightening, stiffening, as if she finally picked up that something was really wrong. A sudden silence stretched between them, awkward and tense. Eventually she seemed to realize that no one was going to break it if she didn't. "It's late, isn't it?"

He leapt onto the innocuous subject like a dog onto a bone. "Yeah. Really late."

Her eyes searched his face, one last time, and then dropped. She rubbed her arms, as if just then noticing the night's damp chill, and bustled up a smile. "Heavens, the time just got completely away from me," she said in a voice spring-loaded with fake cheer. "I'd really better get on the move. I meant to leave hours ago." Her spine was ruler-stiff with pride when she turned around and started walking.

Seth scalped an exasperated hand through his hair. It was exactly what he wanted her to say, that she was leaving, immediately. He didn't need any more tangles with nitroglycerin. Only, tarnation. It just wasn't right.

"Samantha," he called after her. It was the first time he'd used her name, and she turned on a dime. "Look—it would be nuts for you to take off now. Driving anywhere would be dangerous. The fog's thicker than soup, and you're not familiar with the roads. You don't even know where you'd find a place to stay—"

"It doesn't matter. I'll find somewhere."

Not good enough, he thought irritably. Who knew where she'd end up if he let her go? Before, he'd worried about some guy taking advantage of her on the road, but that was imagining. Now he knew for sure that she was a witless, impractical romantic with shaky judgment about men. The potential of her getting into trouble wasn't a maybe. It was a for sure. "I know you have no reason to trust me, but I'm telling you. I won't come on to you again. I swear you'll be safe with me, staying here."

Safe, Samantha thought, was a relative term. An hour later, she closed the door on the blue bedroom, peeled off her clothes and tugged the oversize nightshirt over her head. Once she flicked off the overhead light, the room flooded with eerie shadows. The paneled wall creaked. Floorboards groaned, as if under the weight of a heavy boot print. A whispery draft brushed over her skin.

Ignoring all that—naturally she was susceptible to imagining ghost sounds; it was the whole blasted reason she'd come to this house—she climbed onto the bed, twisted her legs in the lotus position, closed her eyes and mentally began reciting a mantra.

Outside the door, she could hear Seth still moving around. Panther-quiet footsteps between the bathroom and his bedroom. A shiver-low masculine tenor, murmuring to his dog. Then the sound of a door closing, the click of the latch distinctly audible...so noticeably loud that he'd probably meant her to hear it, she mused fretfully. Seth had taken great pains to make sure she knew that her chastity was safe with him.

Her so-called chastity had always been safe. She'd learned to say no early and effectively, because that was her only guaranteed defense against being used. Ambition was genetically inbred in her neighborhood. Boys had started calling before she was out of a training bra. Even the nicest, even the ones with the sweetest faces, got a certain look in their eyes when they crossed the Adams threshold. It wasn't her family's fault that they had money and influence, but Samantha, of necessity, had lost her naïveté quickly. One boy had mistakenly believed that a little forced seduction would further his cause of marrying into the Adams family. Samantha had knocked his block off. Geoff was his name. There had been miles of boys between Geoff and Joe, but she'd never had trouble hanging tight to her virtue. Chastity was about her last goal in life—good grief, virginity was embarrassing at the vast age of twenty-seven—but the stomach-dropping fear of being used was hard to shake. Damned if she was going to risk getting naked with someone who felt more passionately about dollar signs than her.

She'd only met one man, ever, where that fear never even crossed her mind.

"Y'er thinking about Seth, aren't ye, lassie?"

She heard the whiskey-rough masculine voice, and irritably scratched her nose. She didn't have this meditation thing down pat yet. Her imagination never instantly shut off just because she religiously concentrated on a mantra. The trick was simply to concentrate harder on her breathing, not fight the mind's interruptions and just go with the flow.

"Ye wanted him, didn't ye, sweetling? I saw the two of ye in the grass. Ye wanted him like a madness, didn't ye? Ye closed yer eyes and molded to him slick as butter on bread. I know what ye women are taught, but it's naught to be ashamed of. A real man doesna like coyness, and lar, he *is* a real man. Strong and true. He'd watch over you, he would...."

Samantha opened one eye, scratched the tickle of an itch on her right big toe, and then firmly settled back into her deep breathing exercise. Her imagination didn't usually run to monologues in Scottish accents, but it wasn't hard to guess where the thoughts were coming from. She *knew* she'd thrown herself at Seth. She wasn't sure yet what sparked that completely out-of-character behavior when he touched her, but it was seriously mortifying to have acted like a deprived nymphomaniac with a man who was sorry, clearly *dead* sorry, for kissing her. She was still shaken. She needed some time to get a grip.

Meditation was supposed to take her mind off what happened, and by God, she was going to meditate.

"He needs ye, lassie. He's alone. I dona ken what his problem is, but I'll tell ye, it's something he canna handle alone. He's a loving man. Ye can see it in everything he does, but even a strong oak will wither if no exposed to rain and sunlight. Ye could matter to him, lass. Really matter."

With a scowl Samantha opened both eyes. There was, of course, no one in the room. However tempting it was to blame that voice on a ghost, she knew darn well it was coming from the echo of her own heart. That was exactly how she'd felt—that Seth was alone, that he needed someone. There was no magic, no fairy dust, just the soul-deep intuition that he was as wounded by life as she was. When he kissed her, his need to hold and be held, to express love and warmth, had come across so potently that she'd responded with matching honesty and pure emotion.

Was it an illusion that he felt the same way? Lord, she was so confused. She was stuck with a romantic, idealistic nature—the very reason she'd learned to be careful about trust—but maybe reality was simply hormones. Maybe her conscience was just looking for excuses to justify why she'd come on to him like Ms. Ripe and Ready. Maybe he didn't feel a thing for her, and she'd made a perfect fool out of herself. One thing was for sure. Until she sorted it out, she didn't need to hear any more confounded *voices*.

Palms laid up, eyes closed, body still, she started chanting the mantra again. Loudly.

"I want ye to think about laying with him, lass. When ye dream tonight, I want ye to think about him naked with ye. Think about the two of ye on a feather

mattress in the dark, you pinned, him over ye...
claiming ye as sure as a pirate claims treasure, yer
breath coming broken and yer..."

That did it. Heart pounding, both her eyes shot
wide. Any prayer of concentration had gone up in
smoke. She scooted out of the bed, bumped her toe on
the bedside table, tripped to the door and yanked it
open.

The hallway was ebony-black. No light shone beneath Seth's bedroom door. The ancient old house had
been making a dozen settling noises, creaks and clanks
and wind-whistling-through-floorboards sounds, but
there was nothing now. No unexpected sounds. No
voices. No zip. "Jezzie?" she whispered. "Jezebel?"

A huge black shadow loomed from the base of
Seth's bedroom door. Claws clicked on the chestnut
floor. A fat tail thwumped enthusiastically against a
wall.

"Jezzie?" she whispered. "Would you come sleep
with me, baby?"

When Samantha came downstairs the next morning, she found Seth already in the kitchen. A hazy,
watery sun spilled through the windows, shafting on
the tarp-covered floor. Tools and refinishing prod-
ucts lined one counter. The fresh aroma of coffee
wafted from the bubbling pot on the stove, but Seth
wasn't drinking coffee, and he wasn't working, either.

Samantha hesitated, unsure what to say or what his
mood was after the night before. Finally she ventured
a simple "Good morning."

"Morning." He didn't turn around from where he
was hunched down, elbows resting on his knees,

frowning at—as far as she could tell—an extremely innocuous cupboard door. "Samantha, were you in the kitchen last night?"

Whatever she was expecting, it certainly wasn't that totally irrelevant question. "No. Why?"

"You're sure you weren't in the kitchen?"

"Sure I'm sure. What's the problem?"

"Sawdust," he muttered. "Sawdust is the problem."

Samantha rapidly found a cracked cup and poured herself some coffee. Truthfully she rarely drank the brew; herbal teas were more to her taste, but a shot of caffeine was clearly called for. It was undoubtedly because she was still sleepy that his conversation hadn't made a lick of sense so far.

Gulping down a jolting slug of the hot brew, she hunkered down next to him. His jeans had a rip in the knee. His navy blue T-shirt stretched taut over his muscular forearms, and the sun caught the dusting of dark hair on his arms. He hadn't shaved. The whisker stubble on his chin and his tousled hair added to a general disreputable air. He gave off more pure masculine energy than a sexual cyclone, and her feminine nerves tuned straight to that channel. Seth didn't. If he even remembered sharing a wild, unprincipled, winsomely compelling embrace the night before, he sure didn't show it. Beyond a quick glance at her fresh-washed face and neatly brushed hair—a glance and a frown—his attention returned instantly to the thin film of sawdust under the cupboard door.

"I'm not sure," she said delicately, "why you're finding that sawdust so fascinating."

"Because it can't be there. That's why."

"Ahh."

"We stripped the paint off yesterday. That's how it's done. First you strip down to bare wood, then you sand, then you stain or oil or varnish, depending on how you want to finish the wood and what would best show off the natural grain. Only dammit." He sifted sawdust through his fingers. "The wood was still damp yesterday afternoon, not ready to sand, and I didn't touch it. I had rolls of sandpaper with my tools, ready to start work today. Only it's all done. And there's no explanation for the sawdust all over the floor—" he swung around to face her "—unless you came down in the middle of the night and did it."

"Um, Seth? Afraid I wouldn't know sandpaper from a horse's behind. Not that I'm not willing to learn," she offered hastily, "but without asking you first, I wouldn't know beans about how to do anything like that."

"The cupboards didn't sand themselves. It *had* to be you."

"Okay." Why argue with him? She didn't mind taking credit for helping out, especially when the problem was clearly upsetting him. A shock of hair had fallen on his brow. His neck and shoulder muscles were bunched with tension. She wondered what he'd do if she reached over and simply, naturally hugged him, wondered how long it had been since he'd let anyone hug him. Too long, she guessed, but decided right then might not be the wisest moment to test it. "Did you have some breakfast?"

"No. Not yet. As soon as I got downstairs, I...aw, hell." He jerked to his feet as if shot. At first Samantha thought he suddenly realized how close she was, but that hardly explained the redbrick color of embarrassment flushing up his neck. "Don't worry about it. I'll take care of it."

"Take care of what?" The whole morning was taking on the aura of the twilight zone. But then she saw where he was looking. The teensy arachnid scuttled between her feet. Samantha's eyebrows feathered into arched wings. "Are you afraid of spiders?"

"Of course not," he snapped.

She studied him, fascinated. He didn't lie well, undoubtedly because his nature was too honest to ever get practice. Who'd have guessed such a big, strong man could be brought down by such a teensy-weensy thing? "Everyone's afraid of something," she said soothingly, "There's nothing to be embarrassed about."

"I'm not *embarrassed*. Or *afraid*." Fractured masculine ego vibrated in his tone. "It just happened that I was bit once by a brown recluse spider. They're usually fawn colored, sometimes a little darker, with a patch mark on their backs, and they hide out in dark places. The female's more dangerous than the male. I was bitten by a female. Didn't even notice the bite at the time, but about two hours later I had to be carted off in an ambulance. Spent two ridiculous days in a hospital, sick as a dog."

"Well, then, it's perfectly logical that you'd be nervous around spiders," Samantha said calmly. But she thought, damn, Seth, did it have to be a *female* spider who bit you? How many Jezebel-type scars are you carrying around? "That has to be extra hard, though, in your line of work. If you're around wood, you must be stuck coming across spiders all the time."

"Most often I'm working with new construction, and that's no particular sweat. It's just that when you get into older houses like this one, there are a million of them. Spiders come out of the woodwork just like ghosts."

It was just a turn of phrase, but Samantha couldn't help but make the association between she-biting-spiders and Jezebels and ... yeah ... ghosts. In two shakes she found her purse in the hall, fetched a tissue, and bending down, took care of the little devil. She only wished it was that easy to exorcise the female ghosts who seemed to have scarred his heart. "One spider. All gone. You wanna strike a bargain? I'll save you from all the spiders if you'll save me from mice."

"Mice?"

"They give me the willies," she confessed. "I hate setting traps. I don't want to kill them. They're cute. It's just when I see one running across the floor, I have the embarrassing tendency to leap on a chair with the screaming meemies." She cleared her throat. "Seth?"

"Hmm?"

"Since we seem to be confessing our most mortifying phobias, would you please listen to me? I need to be honest with you about something."

From the look on his face, Samantha thought, he'd rather tackle the spider.

This just wasn't going to be easy.

Six

"I don't want you to laugh," Samantha said firmly.

"You just found out I'm a total wuss around spiders. You think I'm gonna laugh at anything you're afraid of?"

"This is different. I'm afraid you won't take me seriously."

"God. Women. Samantha, would you just spit out whatever you want to say?"

"Okay." Samantha took a breath. "I think...I *really* think...there's something in this house. A presence. Not hocus pocus, nothing I'm dreaming up to tease you, but honestly *something*. And I think it's in the blue bedroom upstairs."

The tension seeped out of his shoulders like a deflated balloon. She guessed he'd been afraid she wanted to talk about some nasty, terrifying, upsetting subject like feelings—particularly the kind of emotional and sexual feelings they'd shared the night before. He not only looked relieved that the topic was ghosts, but humor lines crinkled around his eyes. "Give me a break. Come on, Sam."

"I'm serious."

"Sure you are," he said dryly. Scanning the kitchen floor, he spotted his tool belt and promptly strapped it on. He had work to do. He might have postponed it if she needed to talk about something serious, but ghosts didn't qualify.

"I told you about Jock, didn't I?" Samantha persisted. "He's the ghost that's supposed to haunt this house, according to those diaries and letters I told you about. Supposedly he was a pirate. Early 1700s. A crony of Blackbeard's, you know?"

"No, I don't know. Blackbeard...wasn't he the pirate who considered himself God's gift to women?"

"According to some legends, yes. He was a real cutthroat on the seas, but with women he had a reputation for being an irresistible lover. I suppose he came across as brave, reckless, all that stuff. Women have always liked that swept-away-by-a-pirate fantasy."

"Yeah?" His grin died. He definitely didn't want to pursue the subject of "irresistible lovers." "Well, what's all that got to do with your Jock?"

"Jock had the same kind of reputation with women. Physically he was supposed to be kind of short and stocky, with long black curly hair. I thought I saw him in the window outside last night. And later, when I was trying to sleep...I didn't *see* him, Seth, but I swear I heard this voice. A man's voice. A low, baritone, distinctly *man's* voice."

"That's exactly what you wanted, isn't it? To have some kind of confounded experience with . . . um . . . a ghost?"

"Well, yes. Only—"

"Only nothing. You're not going to convince me that you really believe in that nonsense. You *know* what happened. It was dark, this old house makes a hundred settling sounds in the night and you talked yourself into believing that you heard something that wasn't there."

"I'm sure that's true," Samantha admitted, "but . . ."

"But what?"

"But I was scared," she said honestly.

That single word seemed to spin him around. Samantha had a feeling that he'd rather take a beating than discuss what had happened between them the night before. Maybe he thought the attraction between them would disappear if he denied it hard enough, but her admitting to being afraid was clearly a fish of a different species. Seth had a protective streak about women that not even the Jezebels in his life had been able to shake.

"Sweetheart." The use of the endearment might have gone straight to her head, if he hadn't been shaking his with both humor and exasperation. He grabbed her hand. "Come on."

"Come on where?"

"We're going upstairs. To the blue bedroom. Where you think you heard ol' Jock boy."

Seth didn't exactly mean to take her hand. In his view, no man with a brain expected to hike through poison ivy without consequences. Any further physical contact with Samantha was a clear-cut bad risk, but this was different, for cripes sake. She'd apparently talked herself into really being afraid. When he was a shrimp of a kid, he'd been terrified of boogeymen in the closet. He'd stiffed it out, slept without lights and refused to close the damn closet door. But he was a guy. He was supposed to be tough.

Samantha, he already knew, was prey to emotions. Hell, she responded emotionally to just about everything. He had a bad feeling—a disastrous feeling—that if she really loved someone, there was nothing she'd hold back, and worse, that she was building up some heavyweight caring emotions about him. That couldn't happen. It didn't matter how he felt about her. He could never risk failing her as a lover, and that was for *dead* sure. Tackling her boogeymen, though, was a pip-squeak easy project by comparison.

Her palm was small and damp in his. "I know you think this is silly," she said.

"I don't think fear is ever silly." He didn't drop her hand until they reached the doorway of the blue bedroom. Abruptly he changed his mind about tackling her boogeymen.

Her sleeping bag was still laid out on the mattress, rumpled and peeled back, and the pillow still had the imprint of her head. A pair of tiger-print underpants lay on the floor. They looked no bigger than a G-string. The crystal she usually wore was on the bedside table, catching rays of color from the morning sun. She'd cracked a window, apparently because she liked to sleep cold, but the breezy salt air couldn't quite dispel the scent of her, the faint exotic, erotic spicy scent that he'd already come to associate uniquely with her.

Even dressed in a bulky sweatshirt and jeans, she stirred his hormones. Stirred, heat-whipped and ignited his libido like a match tossed into a pool of gasoline. How could he possibly have lost his head with her the night before? *Her?* When he knew damn well where touching her could lead to? He averted his gaze from those tiger-striped underpants right quick.

"No ghosts in sight," he remarked dryly. Bending down, he peered under the bed. Jezebel, who'd followed them up, poked her wet nose under the bed, too. She liked this game. "You see anything, Jezzie?" He lifted his head. "Jezzie doesn't see anything, either," he reported.

Samantha propped her hands on her hips. "I should have known you wouldn't take this seriously."

"Are you kidding? I'm taking your ghost so seriously that I'm going to solve the problem. Watch." As grave as a judge, he walked the length of the north wall, rapping his knuckles in places, listening for hollow spots. Then, looking most thoughtful, he dug a hammer from the back of his tool belt and swung back.

Her jaw dropped when he thwacked the wall, leaving a gaping hole the size of a baseball and plaster dust flying every which way. He used the clawside of the hammer to enlarge the opening. When it was big enough to stick his head in, he did. "I knew there was a hollow space between the two bedrooms. Darned if I know what the architect was thinking of, but now we know for sure there are no ghosts in there, either, right?"

"Connor, I don't believe you! What have you done? You're crazy. You're plumb nuts. You're out of your mind—"

"Well, I can't take *that* much credit." He had to admit he loved the look of shock on her face. So far she'd shocked him plenty—a man could feel keel-hauled-anxious worrying what she was going to do next—but this was the first chance he'd had to turn the tables on her. "That wall was already doomed. Truthfully the hole is a little premature—I doubt I can get to the project until next week, with so much to finish downstairs. But I'd already planned to knock out the sucker. The green bedroom on the other side is just as dinky as this one. Take out the wall between the two rooms, and the combined space would make a heck of an upstairs living room. Big enough for a media center, a couple of couches, maybe a wet sink in the corner. The view of the ocean would be terrific from up here, much better than any room on the first floor. More to the point..."

He slugged the hammer back into its belt holster, dusted his hands and grinned. "More to the point, it solves your problem, honey. If you wanna study ghosts, you can study ghosts, but now you won't have to sleep with one. For as long as you're here, you can camp in the bedroom next to mine. No ghosts are going to bother you there—trust me—and I really don't think they're going to bother me when I'm in the middle of a construction project."

Seth was the first man who'd torn down walls for her. The first to kiss her senseless and not even try to take advantage. The first and only man she'd known who never let sexual chemistry distract him from doing what he thought was right. Samantha had the perilous, exhilarating, terrifying feeling that she was already falling in love with him.

Getting him to go out to dinner, however, was an uphill job. Cajoling didn't accomplish much. He was obviously content working himself to exhaustion on the house. The whole time she was taking rookie-varnishing lessons, working side by side with him in the kitchen, she'd tried subtle hints. He was deaf to subtle hints. The only thing that finally worked—she should have guessed—was the mournful, woebegone plea that she was starving to death.

Guilt was an extraordinary motivator with Seth. Even with a shower and a change of clothes, he had her packed into the Firebird on the short side of twenty minutes.

It was early for the dinner crowd in Bar Harbor. When the waitress escorted them upstairs, they were alone in the second-floor dining room. Windows wrapped around the ocean view, showing off a bruise blue sky and a harbor jammed with a mixture of working-fishermen's boats and expensive sail craft.

When the curly-haired waitress handed out bibs, Seth looked so startled that she had to chuckle. "You haven't had lobster before?"

"The menu where I grew up in Colorado ran more toward canned beef stew and la spaghetti." Seth took the bib, but he didn't put it on. He was still looking over the place, as if unsure what kind of fancy deal she'd conned him into. The floor was plain planks, the tables wood, the place set up for serious lobster eaters. When he saw no white linens or tuxedoed waiters, he started to relax.

"Colorado? I thought you were from Atlanta?"

He ordered a bottle of dark ale. A few sips of that, and he relaxed a little more. "I moved to Atlanta around ten years ago. Back then, the city was having a construction boom and there was no end of work for a good carpenter. The boom's long over—in fact, a lot of people in construction folded like a house of cards, but I hung on. Actually I expanded. Four people working for me. We do okay."

"You have two brothers, right?" Samantha pulled apart a steaming roll and lavished butter on it. "Are they still in Colorado?"

"No. We're split up all over the country. Zach—he's the youngest—he headed for L.A. He just got married around Christmas and they have a baby on the way. Music's his field. He's beyond good. I swear he can make a saxophone talk. And Michael...he's three years older than I am. Moved to Michigan years ago, Grosse Pointe, owns a couple of tool-and-die plants, some property. He was born loving business. Put a dollar in his hand and he'll double it faster than you can blink. I'm the only one who settled into doing anything...ordinary."

The way he said "ordinary" made Samantha glance up. "Don't you love what you do?"

"Sure. But it's straight blue collar. Nothing like what my brothers have accomplished."

Samantha wanted to argue—it sounded as if he was putting himself down—but it was the first time he'd willingly talked about his family. His pride and love for his brothers was as clear as a diamond, but so far she'd never heard him refer, even once, to any female members of his clan. "No girls in your family?"

A dry smile. "None. The Connor men aren't exactly known for luck with women. I can't even remember one being around. My grandfather—the one who willed us that albatross of a house—was married and divorced three times. My dad didn't have any better luck. Mom left us for greener pastures when I was knee high. Dad raised the three of us single-handed.''

"No wonder you grew up on beef stew and canned spaghetti,'' Samantha murmured.

"Drastically different than your family, I'll bet.''

Abruptly Samantha guessed why he'd been so openly chit-chatting about his background. It was a chance for him to illustrate how little they had in common. She'd surely think twice about becoming too interested in a guy who was straight blue collar, no silver spoon in his mouth, raised on canned food, now would she?

God, she would. When the waitress delivered the platter of steaming lobsters, Samantha dived straight in, but her mind lingered on the facts he'd shared. Her heart pictured a motherless little boy, growing up in a family where the only females either cheated or deserted ship. It was no wonder he'd fallen prey to a Jezebel. His judgment about women had undoubtedly been colored by his past.

Their backgrounds *were* different, Samantha mused, but not in everything. The more she learned about him, the more she understood why she'd felt such a natural, kindred spirit draw for him from the beginning. Her relationships with the opposite sex had made her wary of trust, just as his had. And she knew exactly what it felt like to be the family misfit, to feel "ordinary" compared to a clan of massive over-achievers.

"I'll ask the waitress to get you another drink if you're thirsty...." His voice trailed off. Initially when the lobster arrived, he'd followed her lead, cracking the shell with pinchers and using the mini fork to pull out the meat. He seemed concerned about the etiquette of a lobster dinner. She'd already told him that manners in such an instance didn't apply.

"What's wrong?" she asked him.

"Nothing." But he leveled a slug of beer before trying to eat again, and then he stopped all over again to watch her.

She loved lobster. Truthfully she loved food in any form, and her particular metabolism demanded a lot of it. But eating lobster was inevitably a physical experience. A sensual experience. She speared a long tidbit of the shellfish, dipped it in butter and tore into it with her teeth. Beads of sweat appeared on Seth's brow.

"Is it too warm in here?" she asked him.

"No. The temperature's fine."

Truthfully she thought it was, too. Several windows were pushed up, letting in a delectably cool breeze off the ocean. "Don't you like it? We can order something else. I only tried to talk you into trying the lobster because you said you'd liked other kinds of shellfish before—"

"It's fine. Very good. It's just . . . do you always eat lobster like that?"

"Like what?" She forked another wedge of white meat, dredged it in the hot melted butter and popped it between her parted lips. More beads of sweat formed on Seth's forehead. He ran a finger in the collar of his shirt, as if the material were suddenly too tight. "Eating lobster's messy. There's no way around it. You might as well just go with the flow and enjoy it. Are you having trouble getting it up?"

"*What?*"

IT'S FREE!

MAN! BIG BUCK$

HOW TO PLAY

It's so easy...grab a lucky coin, and go right to your BIG BUCKS game card. Scratch off silver squares in a STRAIGHT LINE (across, down, or diagonal) until 5 dollar signs are revealed. BINGO...Doing this makes you eligible for a chance to win $1,000,000.00 in lifetime income ($33,333.33 each year for 30 years)! Also scratch all 4 corners to reveal the dollar signs. This entitles you to a chance to win the $50,000.00 Extra Bonus Prize! Void if more than 9 squares scratched off.

Your EXCLUSIVE PRIZE NUMBER is in the upper right corner of your game card. Return your game card and we'll activate your unique Sweepstakes Number, so it's important that your name and address section is completed correctly. This will permit us to identify you and match you with any cash prize rightfully yours! (SEE BACK OF BOOK FOR DETAILS.)

FREE BOOKS PLUS FREE GIFTS!

At the same time you play your BIG BUCKS game card for BIG CASH PRIZES...scratch the Lucky Charm to receive FOUR FREE

Silhouette Desire® novels, and a FREE GIFT, TOO! They're totally free, absolutely free with no obligation to buy anything!

These books have a cover price of $2.99 each. But THEY ARE TOTALLY FREE; even the shipping will be at our expense! The Silhouette Reader Service™ is not like some book clubs. You don't have to make any minimum number of purchases–not even one!

The fact is, thousands of readers look forward to receiving six of the best new romance novels each month and they love our discount prices!

Of course you may play BIG BUCKS for cash prizes alone by not scratching off your Lucky Charm, but why not get everything that we are offering and that you are entitled to! You'll be glad you did.

Offer limited to one per household and not valid to current Silhouette Desire® subscribers. All orders subject to approval.

TWO WAYS TO WIN BIG BUCKS!

EXCLUSIVE PRIZE # 40 197607

BIG BUCKS

$

HURRY!
This jackpot must be claimed!

Scratch here →

LUCKY CHARM GAME!

Charm
4 FREE Books
AND a FREE
Mystery Gift!

225 CIS ANTL
(U-SIL-D-05/94)

YES! I have played my BIG BUCKS game card as instructed. Enter my Big Bucks Prize number in the MILLION DOLLAR Sweepstakes III and also enter me for the Extra Bonus Prize. When winners are selected, tell me if I've won. If the Lucky Charm is scratched off, I will also receive everything revealed, as explained on the back of this page.

NAME _____

ADDRESS _____ APT. ____

CITY _____ STATE _____ ZIP _____

NO PURCHASE OR OBLIGATION NECESSARY TO ENTER SWEEPSTAKES.

PRINTED IN U.S.A.

© 1993 HARLEQUIN ENTERPRISES LTD.

1. Uncover 5 $ signs in a row . . . BINGO! You're eligible to win the $1,000,000.00 SWEEPSTAKES!

2. Uncover 5 $ signs in a row AND uncover $ signs in all 4 corners . . . BINGO! You're also eligible for the $50,000.00 EXTRA BONUS PRIZE!

THE SILHOUETTE READER SERVICE™: HERE'S HOW IT WORKS

Accepting free books places you under no obligation to buy anything. You may keep the books and gift and return the shipping statement marked "cancel". If you do not cancel, about a month later we will send you 6 additional novels and bill you just $2.44 each plus 25¢ delivery and applicable sales tax, if any.* That's the complete price, and – compared to cover prices of $2.99 each – quite a bargain! You may cancel at any time, but if you choose to continue, every month we'll send you 6 more books, which you may either purchase at the discount price...or return at our expense and cancel your subscription.

*Terms and prices subject to change without notice. Sales tax applicable in N.Y.

BUSINESS REPLY MAIL
FIRST CLASS MAIL   PERMIT NO. 717   BUFFALO, NY

POSTAGE WILL BE PAID BY ADDRESSEE

"BIG BUCKS"
MILLION DOLLAR SWEEPSTAKES III
3010 WALDEN AVE.
P.O. BOX 1867
BUFFALO, NY 14240-9952

NO POSTAGE
NECESSARY
IF MAILED
IN THE
UNITED STATES

She blinked. "I meant, are you having trouble getting the meat up. Sometimes it's hard to get it out of the shell. Do you want me to help you?"

"No. Thanks. No. I'm...um...doing fine." He muttered, "I just think that if someone made a movie of you eating, it'd be banned in Boston."

"Pardon?" She wasn't sure she'd heard him correctly.

"I said—" he cleared his throat "—that my sister-in-law claims Maine lobsters are better than Boston's."

"I don't know. But it's hard to believe there's anything better than this. Of course," she admitted, "I love food."

"Yeah, I know."

He seemed to intuitively know other things about her, Samantha mused. It was late when they drove home, but she wasn't ready to be cooped up in the house yet. Seth suggested a walk before she even asked.

The moon was just rising as they ambled toward the beach. Jezebel joined them, happy they were home. Waves slurped onto the shore, making the boulders glisten like polished ebony. In the distance the deserted lighthouse loomed, tall and round, pure white, a romantic symbol of light in a night of darkness. She caught Seth looking at it.

"Makes you think of pirates and shipwrecks and wild storms, doesn't it?" she murmured.

"Your imagination runs a little wilder than mine," he said dryly, but admitted, "I keep meaning to explore it. It's locked, but there's a key somewhere in the house. We'll get to it."

Samantha noted that "we" and wondered if he had consciously included her, but she didn't press. Neither of them talked much. They hiked for more than an hour, tromping over rocks, dawdling near the surf edge, mutually savoring the soporific ocean sounds and the ever-darkening night.

Finally, though, the huge dinner and walk caught up with her, and she had to stifle a yawn. "I think I'm going to turn in. Are you coming?"

"Not quite yet."

He was as beat as she was—there were bruised shadows of tiredness under his eyes—but Samantha understood that he wanted to give her the chance to get ready for bed first. He avoided going upstairs at the same time with her, particularly now that she was sleeping in the bedroom next to his. But he'd also made a point, several times, of telling her she could stay until she finished her "research." Samantha was increasingly captivated by the pirate ghost haunting the house, but she could hardly tell Seth that the ghosts who haunted him interested her far more. Maybe it was wrong to stay. Maybe it was a crazy, dangerous risk, especially for a woman who had always guarded her heart against loving any man who didn't love her in return.

Yet if she left now, she had no doubt that she would never see Seth again. It was either take a chance, or have that chance disappear forever. She'd never felt this strange feeling of richness and excitement with anyone else. She could laugh with him, be quiet with him, be *herself* with him. More, the sureness kept building that she could make a difference for Seth. Every woman wasn't like his Jezebel. They'd shared honesty, laughter, understanding. She wouldn't hurt him. She thought—hoped—he was beginning to believe that.

When he walked her back as far as the porch, he stopped, obviously intending to wait until she was safely inside. "Seth? Thanks for dinner."

"De nada."

Impulsively she touched his sleeve and then lifted up to brush his cheek. No more. He was clearly uneasy about the sexual chemistry between them; she wasn't sure what she should do about that, what she shouldn't, what he honestly wanted, what he didn't. Still, he surely wouldn't object to a gesture of honest affection.

The brush of a kiss only lasted seconds. Her fingertips trailed his cheek. Their lips never connected; her breasts never touched his chest; her whole body never swayed toward him, although the lonesome, winsome magnet pull was there. She wasn't the only one feeling the rush of desire. For an instant, she could see the burn of his eyes in the darkness, blue-black, liquid fire.

He clutched her hand for a pulsebeat. Maybe it was the night's spell of moonbeams and stardust that infected him at the moment, but it was the first time he'd voluntarily touched her. The press of his palm expressed that he wanted her. That he needed her. That maybe, just maybe, he felt the same heady brew of a love potion that she did.

As quickly as he dropped her hand, she turned toward the house.

She didn't want to do anything to break that spell. However small the gesture, his reaching out implied the first fragile tendril of trust. He had feelings for her. Feelings he was no longer trying to deny, and her heart

sensed how rare and hard that was for him to reveal.
She already knew that trust was a mountain for Seth
to cross with any woman.

She vowed not to do anything—even the smallest
thing—to make him nervous around her again.

Seth was carrying two pails of spackling compound
upstairs when the telephone rang. The closest receiver
was in his bedroom, which he had to hustle to reach by
the fourth ring. The caller was his youngest brother.

"Zach? How's it going? I haven't talked with you
in over a week...no, I've been around. I was just gone
for an hour to the hardware store. Sorry I missed
you...."

He caught a glimpse of neon orange from the window. Twisting the phone cord, he angled closer to the
French doors to see what it was. Edgy nerves immediately pooled low in his stomach.

"...No, I finished the kitchen yesterday. It took a
long week, but she spiffed up great. All she really
needed was a face-lift. Once the cupboards were re-
finished and I changed the lighting..."

Dammit, what kind of woman sunbathed sur-
rounded by a library of books? Psychic books, he'd
bet. She'd spread out a blanket on the stretch of a
round flat rock, high over the sheltered lee of the cove.
Jezzie was with her. Jezebel was darn near inseparable from her. Seth could see strands of her black hair
whispering in the wind. He could see pages of books—
she seemed to have circled herself with tomes—flut-
tering in the breeze. He could see she was wearing an
orange bikini. A hot-orange, disgraceful scrap of a
bikini, and damnation and tarnation, she was only
wearing the bottoms.

Seth scalped a hand through his hair. "...I hit the hardware store, because I plan to start on the upstairs this afternoon. I put a hole in the wall last week, but just haven't had a chance to get up there since. This project'll take me a little longer. Ten days, for sure. I have to put up drywall and even out the floor..."

He couldn't see her breasts, because her back was turned to him, but he could see the bare, long slope of her spine. Golden. Smooth. Feminine. No one else could see her. Bright sailboats were skimming the horizon and beachcombers were shambling down the shoreline in the distance, but this strip of land was private and she was perched way up high on those rocks. Technically she was only exposing herself to the sun, sky and Jezzie.

Not him.

She couldn't *know* that he'd see her. For one thing, she thought he was still at the hardware store. For another, even if he'd returned, she'd think he was working in the blue bedroom because that's where he'd told her he would be. She had no reason to think he'd be standing in the French doors of his bedroom in the middle of the day, which was the only place—except for the roof—that he'd conceivably get a look at her.

"Seth?"

"Hmm?" Belatedly he realized that he'd lost track of his brother's conversation.

"I didn't call just to talk about your construction plans. I called to ask how you were doing."

"Fine. Just fine."

"You haven't noticed anything...strange...in the house? A little unusual? Nothing out of the ordinary happen?"

"Haven't had time for anything but work," Seth said flatly. An outright lie. *She'd* happened to him, and was still happening to him. Samantha was under his skin like an unbudgeable nettle. The woman was never going to get her outlandish research done if she kept pitching in to help him. She was always *there*, being funny and interesting and maddeningly easy to be with. Seth had told himself a dozen times that she was absolutely nothing like any woman he'd ever been drawn to, but damned if it didn't jab like a razor cut, that if things were different, he might have fallen in love with her.

Maybe he already was.

He was tempted to take up that hoaxy meditation she was into. Possibly a steady mantra of *"can't"* would eventually brand some sense in his brain. The way she ate, the way she walked, the way she smiled—hell, the way she breathed—all sent his hormones keening and charged up his libido like the humming buzz of a bee. She wanted him. It was in her eyes, that she liked him, that she cared, that she was seriously interested. He'd imagined making love to her. He'd imagined showing her, definitively, indelibly, that he didn't give a damn about her money or her family connections like those other jerks. She was precious and vulnerable and beautiful. In bed, he could prove that to her. Over a long dark night, he could illustrate exactly how special and unique and unforgettable she was.

Only it could never happen. It was damn hard to believe that he would wilt with her—she laid a fire in his blood, being anywhere near her—but it could happen. It *had* happened. He'd failed to satisfy Gail, flunked the performance test with another woman. He'd never been as inhibited as Samantha, never as wild, never as naturally sensuous and passionate as she was. Sure, he'd risk making love again sometime. But not with her. Not with a woman where the stakes were too painfully high. He'd die and go to masculine-ego-hell if he failed Samantha....

"Seth? Are you still there? Is something wrong?"

"I'm here. Everything's fine." He clawed a hand through his hair again. Hell, even thinking about her aroused his body to a stinging-aware hardness. Deliberately he turned away from the view through the French doors. "How's Kirstin and the new pregnancy?" he asked jovially.

Zach's new bride was fine. After sharing family news for a few more minutes, Seth ended the phone conversation and clicked down the receiver. He took a long breath, thinking about the bedroom project ahead of him. It was exactly what he needed right now. Work. A sweat job. The kind of physically exhausting, dirty, wear-him-out hard work that both demanded and guaranteed his complete concentration.

He picked up the pails of spackling compound and stalked down the hall. Just inside the door of the blue bedroom, though, he dropped the heavy pails with a startled thud.

The wall, of course, had a hole. He'd put it there himself a week ago, and Samantha had been right there as a witness. The hole had been as big as a basketball. Far too huge for anyone to ignore or imagine.

Only, now, there was nothing there. He stared at the wall disbelievingly. The surface wasn't exactly smooth. A scar in the plaster testified to the walloping hole he'd made, but it just plain wasn't there now.

"Samantha!"

Seven

"It wasn't me."

"It had to be you."

Samantha shook her head. "I think it was the ghost. Maybe for some reason he doesn't want you messing with that blue bedroom."

"Samantha, that's ridiculous."

Stretched out on the threadbare Oriental carpet in the parlor, her back against the horsehair couch, she reached for the bowl of popcorn. They'd already had dinner, listened to Tom Brokaw's version of the day's disasters and hashed through this about a dozen times. Talking hadn't helped. Seth was still pacing the room like a bear with a sore paw. "I had no possible motivation for fixing your wall," she reminded him again. "I think your idea about combining the two rooms is terrific. And anyway, I'd never have interfered. How would I know how to fix a hole in a wall?"

"Well, *someone* fixed that stupid wall."

She munched on the buttery popcorn, trying to come up with another theory. "Maybe you fixed it yourself in your sleep. All kinds of people sleepwalk—"

"Not *me*."

"Hmm." A clear strikeout. She tried another pitch. "There's a house in Norway, down near Auburn. A few years ago a couple with a baby bought the place. Things kept happening in the baby's room. Once it started raining in the middle of the night, the parents went in to close the window and it was already closed. Another time the baby cried, and the grandma went upstairs and saw a cat being thrown out of the crib. They brought in a psychic, and it seems that years ago a baby had died in that room, and this ghost was determined to protect their little one—"

"Is that *another* story out of those books you've been reading?"

"Sure is." She watched Seth flop in an overstuffed Morris chair and then bounce back up. He'd changed from his work clothes into clean sweats, but his hair was disheveled and his feet bare. She thought he looked adorable. He kept pinching the bridge of his nose in an expression of comical bedevilment. His fixed wall wasn't *really* causing him stress—not like an earthquake or fire or a real disaster. Those, Samantha suspected, he could handle blindfolded. Grappling with the unexplained and unknown, though, was enough to put a burr in his behind.

He had a heck of a cute behind in those sweats. Samantha guessed she could divert his mind from the problem easily enough if she patted his fanny and kissed him. Right now, though, didn't seem quite the

time. When she'd walked into the house that afternoon in her bikini, he'd dropped a sweatshirt over her
head that was a size bigger than a shroud. Seth clearly
wasn't in the mood for teasing—at least the kind of
teasing that involved body contact.

"Even assuming there is a ghost," she said
thoughtfully, "there's no reason to believe the spirit is
malevolent. Ghosts can be good guys, so to speak. Did
you ever see *The Ghost and Mrs. Muir?* Or *Topper*
with Cary Grant?"

"No. But I'll bet five bucks they were both sappy
love stories."

"Movies to die for," she agreed, "but since you're
not familiar with films, we might as well move on.
There's a whole history of ghosts who had a terrific
time haunting people's lives. The Romans—like Plutarch and Pliny, you know?—they used to believe in
manes. Manes were the type of ghosts who wandered
the earth for the sole purpose of interfering in human
lives. If I remember my research, though, there are a
couple of sure ways to get rid of them—"

"Don't tell me how, okay? Please?"

She cared about him. How could she be less than
helpful? "You can beat drums in the vicinity of the
hauntings," she said with deadpan seriousness. "Or
you can burn black beans. Apparently manes are really allergic to the noxious fumes of black beans—"

A pillow sailed across the room. A couch pillow,
one of those old-fashioned crocheted jobs faded from
a hundred years of wear. It flopped on her head and
then bounced onto her lap, nearly upsetting the whole
popcorn bowl on Jezebel's tummy—who'd been
snoozing next to her through the whole discussion. "I
guess you're not ready to try the black beans, hmm?

And something tells me there isn't going to be a reference for ghost busters in the Yellow Pages. I suppose I could research some other options. Maybe there's someone locally who knows more about the history of the house. I could ask around."

"If you want to ask about history, go ahead. But if you start asking strangers about ghosts, somebody's gonna lock you up in a little room with barred windows."

"I'll be tactful," she promised him.

"When potatoes grow green. You're just putting me on. Again. You know darn well it wasn't a ghost that fixed that wall."

"Okay."

"There is no such thing as manes, ghosts or any other kind of spirits."

"Okay."

He stopped pacing. "You only talk up this psychic nonsense because you know it gets my goat."

"True," Samantha admitted without a qualm. She didn't say what was in her heart. She fed him nonsense, because that was what he seemed to need and want from her. He'd almost laughed when she started talking about burning black beans. Laughter was the most healing medicine she knew. More and more, she thought he was putting that Jezebel in his life out of his mind. If it took ghosts to make him forget her, Samantha was more than willing to bring them up. Seth just wasn't one to believe in things he couldn't touch, hear, see.

She was. There was magic everywhere in life, she believed. But getting Seth to believe that—to feel it— was just a tiny bit tricky. "I think you need to get out of this house," she informed him. "You've been working like a dog. And I know you only have so much time to fix the place up, but a few hours playing hooky wouldn't kill you.''

''What'd you have in mind?''

An afternoon's hike in Acadia was her proposed plan, but it took her two days to talk him into it. Temporarily he dropped the blue bedroom project— to her amusement, he *really* didn't want to go near that room—but he only switched gears to something else. The upstairs hall had a chestnut floor that needed sanding and refinishing. Talk about messes. The sander he rented was noisier than a 747 and raised dust in the whole house; no one could walk upstairs once he started varnishing and the product reeked to high heavens.

More to the point, he was working himself to exhaustion. Samantha finally said it was okay; she'd go to Acadia alone; she'd only been badly lost in the park twice before; a ranger had found her both times so she'd be fine and he didn't need to worry about her.

The fibs worked wonders. He immediately said that they both needed a break, as if the idea had been all his.

Seth drove. Jezebel was a good truck rider, as long as she got the seat next to the window, but the dog took so much space that Samantha was inevitably jammed tight against Seth's thigh. He didn't notice, she thought. For days now, he'd been treating her like a tag-along kid sister.

Working with him, being with him every day, she felt nothing remotely related to sisterly feelings for him. Trust, though, could never be won overnight, and it truly wasn't the kind of day to be too serious about anything. The Acadian coast was peppered with small towns and fishing villages, but the heart of the park itself was primitively wild. Ancient white pines and spruce towered to the sky. Steep rocky inclines led down to yellow sand beaches. There were no roads. No ghosts in sight either, Samantha mused, and the sky was an unbearably sharp blue, cloudless, with dots of colorful sails on the shoreline. Jezebel was in heaven. So was she.

Frisky, gamboling like a colt, she spun around for every wildflower. This early in spring, the bristly red oak leaves had a sting of a smell. Yellow lady's slipper was just starting to bud, so were the golden mustards. She had to search close to find buttercups. Wild geraniums were everywhere, though, bursting any spot they could catch a drink of sun. Jezebel sniffed wherever she did. Seth kept shaking his head, as if wondering how he'd gotten stuck with two equally batty companions.

They chose a trail with no idea where it would take them. The ranger claimed it was a three-mile circle, which Seth worried was too long for her to handle, particularly when she seemed determined to wear herself out in the first three hundred yards. Just because she was wearing safari print shorts and tennies with neon orange laces was no reason to think she lacked practical stamina—which she told him—and as the ranger promised, they had the trail to themselves.

Deep gloomy woods led to a climb on cratery rocks and a flash of sunlit coast. The path eventually twisted up to a plateau. A top-of-the-world plateau. Samantha took in a breathful of ocean air, then scrambled farther. The trail led her to a peninsula of rocks that jutted straight into the ocean with waves splashing on three sides.

She made it to the end, yanked off her backpack, and promptly crashed flat on her back. The rock beneath her was sun-warmed. She inhaled the susurrant breeze and somnolent beat of the sun. Seth dropped down next to her. "I'm never leaving here," she announced.

"I already figured I was going to have to piggyback you out."

"I'm whipped, I'm beat, I'm dead," she confessed.

"What do you expect, when you hike two miles at Kentucky Derby speeds. I told you to slow down, but would you listen?"

"You're not even winded," she said with disgust.

"I'm a guy. We're all tough. It's a rule."

She had to grin. "Well, tough guy, there's a thermos of iced tea in the backpack. I don't suppose you'd be willing to apply your superior strength to pouring us both a cup?"

He rummaged in the sack behind her head. She heard him unscrewing the thermos top. "What kind of tea is this? It smells weird."

"Don't be so suspicious. It's just ginseng. Great for a natural plug of energy. Actually—" she opened one eye "—the Chinese have believed for about a million centuries that ginseng increases a man's virility. Kind of an aphrodisiac, you know?"

With pure innocent pleasure, she watched him choke on the first sip. He recovered all too quickly. "Where'd you pick up that tidbit? One of your ghost books?"

"Heck, no. I read that in a book on herbal love potions."

"Now why doesn't that surprise me?" he asked Jezebel. It surprised Samantha, though, the way he suddenly looked at her, then at that tea. With a most peculiar expression on his face, he gulped down a full cup. "I worked up a serious thirst," he said defensively.

She had, too. There was nothing to feel defensive about. She leaned up on an elbow to sip at the cup he handed her, but the unexpected color in his face still had her perplexed. She'd mentioned the aphrodisiac lore as a joke, guessing it'd be sure fuel for a teasing, but his easy grin had disappeared faster than a cloud blocking the sun. She lifted the thermos. "Do you want some more?"

"No. Is this the part of the park where you were camping out a few weeks ago?"

Samantha recognized a deliberate change of subjects when she heard one. "Not exactly this spot. But it was like this—hilly and wild, lots of woods and rocks."

He lay back, stuffing a sweatshirt under his head for a pillow, one leg cocked up. "I heard you on the telephone last night, talking with your family. You must miss them by now. Your family, your friends and home...maybe even that Joe."

"I miss my family, yes. Not Joe. I don't need to run into any more men who mix love and ambition. It wasn't just him, Seth. Before Joe, there was Geoff and John Timson and Frederick and Baker Forsyth the Third and—"

"Holy kamoly, how many men have been in your life?"

"Enough to stay a runaway for a long time," she said wryly. She kicked off her shoes and wriggled her toes in the sunlight. "There were some things I didn't tell you. Those short jobs I had . . . I started out wait-ressing, and ended up night manager. With the fund-raising thing, I started as a minimum wage paper stuffer, and ended up handling the whole kit and ka-boodle. In spite of myself, I discovered that responsi-bility is catching. It's like the plague. Dangerously infectious."

"And that's bad?"

"Of course it's bad. You can get sucked into the vacuum before you can stop it. Before a woman knows what's happening, she could find herself wearing gray flannel suits and driving station wagons and a whole season of roses gone by before she took the time to smell even one."

"Adams?"

"Hmm?"

"I'm never sure when to believe you. You hand out so much convoluted horseradish that it's almost im-possible to figure out when you're serious."

"You want me to be serious?"

"Occasionally it'd be a nice treat," he said dryly.

She was used to his teasing by now. Even so, she turned on her side, bending an elbow to cuff her cheek in a palm. Who knew when the breeze had shifted? She'd been so sure that Seth didn't want anything but convoluted nonsense from her, that he'd run for the hills if she honestly expressed how she felt about life, about him. But he was relaxed now, the breeze ruf-fling his hair, his eyes half-closed under the sun's warmth. He was easy with her, as he'd never been at the beginning. Surely it was time to take a risk? "If you want me to be serious," she said gently, "I'd like to talk about the small problem of building dynamite between us."

"Dynamite?" His eyes shot wide open, a striking blue against his deeply tanned skin. It was there in his eyes. The instant he realized how close she was. Desire, simmering like a blue hot flame; desire and need and all the emotions he hid so carefully from her.

"Yeah, dynamite. If I touch you, even accidentally," she said softly, "your eyes darken to slate. I've caught you looking at me...the same embarrassing way you've probably caught me looking at you. There's wanting there. As far as I can tell, an explosive ton of it, anytime either of us are even in the same room."

He didn't deny it. She thought Seth wasn't the kind of man to ever deny a problem just because it made him feel uncomfortable. "I'm older than you," he said gruffly. "Old enough to know that nature has a sick sense of humor and can set it up so that hormones never pop up at convenient times."

"You think the only source of that dynamite is hormones?"

"I think that we're from two different parts of the country. And that neither of us have plans to stay in Maine for very long."

"So you're not a fan of short-term flings? Neither am I. But, Seth, no one knows what's going to last. No two people can ever know what a relationship is worth unless they try it on and see how it fits for size."

"Where I grew up, you didn't dive off the edge until you were sure the water was deep enough."

"But how would you ever know that if you didn't test the waters?" She wasn't touching him, yet he was already starting to tense up as if she had. The glint of alarm and anxiety in his eyes was familiar. There'd always been something more serious holding him back than fears of a short ride on the A train. "Seth...what was her name?"

"Whose name?"

"The name of the woman who hurt you. Would it help at all to talk about her?"

"Now where did you get a cockamamy idea like that? Who said I was even involved with a woman?"

So, she thought, the wounds were still that raw, that deep. And though she'd sworn never to take another foolish risk with a man, her heart responded to Seth from sheer feminine instinct. "What if," she said gently, "you got involved with someone who wasn't asking anything from you. What if you took a time-out from life with someone who just made you feel good. What if nothing happened except that you made some memories together, good memories, good feelings, that hurt absolutely no one—"

"You're starting to scare me, Samantha. Now cut this out. From what you said, you took off because you felt pushed against a wall, confused about what you wanted. Everyone loses their way sometimes. You think I don't know what that feels like? But otherwise, you wouldn't be saying any of this—"

"Yeah, I would."

"Then you're even more of a cockeyed romantic than I thought you were. Nothing works out like that in real life. When you get involved with someone, things get messy."

"What if they didn't have to? What if you were only going to feel this way once in your life, and the chance would disappear forever if you didn't take it?" She leaned over him. Her palm brushed his chest. "Your heart is beating so hard. What's going to happen if you kiss me, Connor? Is the world going to cave in? Are you really going to risk some terrible thing if you just give in to that impulse?''

It was either kiss her or shoot her. Seth suspected nothing less would shut her up. But a gun wasn't handy and she could tempt a saint with that sleepy whisper and those velvet black eyes. So, yeah, he kissed her. But when he leveled his mouth on hers, his mood was exasperated and impatient and edgy and had absolutely nothing to do with desire.

God, what a lie.

She *had* to quit playing around with him. Nice girls didn't tease. If no one had ever taught her that before, he would, and mean and roughly if that's what it took to get the message across.

Another lie.

His mouth collided with hers in a crooked, awkward landing, but it didn't seem to matter. He angled his head and the second time their lips connected, it was like a glue-tight bond of a brand. He saw the dark liquid in her eyes, the darkness of need, the liquid of passion, and it seemed to be for him.

If she wasn't every man's dream, she was his. The voltage crackling through his whole body came straight from her. He pushed the scarf from her hair. Warm from the sun, her hair felt silky and slippery as it sieved through his fingers. That second kiss blurred into a third, then another and another, each wilder than the last, each deeper, darker. He pulled her on top of him to save her from being crushed, afraid his weight would hurt her, but then every pulse point in her body came in direct contact with his.

He didn't believe she wanted a fast affair. Didn't believe it for a minute. She didn't mean half of what she told him—he'd long figured out that she hid a lot of vulnerability behind her breezy, sassy ways—but one thing she'd said was terrifyingly true. He'd never felt this way with anyone else and he was soul-sure, heart-sure, that there'd never be anyone like her again. He wasn't really Adam to her Eve; the sun wasn't really shining just for them, but damned if he didn't feel that every moment wasn't precious when he was with her.

Magic. It had her heartbeat. The touch of her, taste of her, feel of her aroused him far beyond reason or sense. Sun shot gold through the curtain of her hair as he skimmed kisses down her jaw, down her throat. It wasn't enough. He pulled her blouse free from her shorts, needing to see her, feel her. *Hurry* was the mantra in his head. Just like magic, he was afraid she would disappear, that this huge, hot hunger would go up in smoke if he didn't touch all of her and soon.

He twisted around when he had her blouse up and open. Her breasts were pearl white in the naked sunlight, firm and plump and gratifyingly responsive to the slightest caress from him. The tips tightened to hard, polished buttons under the warm wash of his tongue. Her hands, just as greedy, tugged and pushed at his sweatshirt. She found damp skin and a fistful of hair on his chest. Her elbow tangled with his. Ten pounds of clothes seemed to be in their way, and Seth knew they needed to slow down. Her slim thighs clamped around his leg, bucking tight; her breath started coming rough and whispery-hoarse, and any prayer of slowing down fled like a tinker's promise.

All those men in her life. He forced himself to remember them. His fear of inadequacy, of failing her,
of wilting and failing to perform—that nightmare was
never far from his mind. But there had to be something in that ginseng tea. Maybe that damn herb had
something toxic in it, something that could make a
man believe he could lie down in a bed of coals and be
perfectly happy burning up. Anxiety thrummed
through his pulse. Powerful anxiety.

It didn't stop the blistering heat from firing through
his blood. Her shorts had an elastic waistband that
bunched when he pushed at it. He twisted around,
leaning over her with one forearm under her head, his
other hand sliding, searing down the length of her,
down, past that bunched waistband, past a scrap of
satin and lace. There was only one answer. Pleasing
her. He could please her without taking her, the risk
to him nonexistent if he didn't have to worry about
failing, and he needed to please her. He needed her to
know that he wasn't like those guys who'd used her;
he needed her to feel loved, for herself, just for herself. Her eyes opened, blurry and luminous and all
unfocused when his rough palm cupped her.

"Seth," she whispered. Even her voice was an ache,
filled with yearning, lonely yearning, calling to something in him that was lonely and yearning, too. Her
teeth closed on his shoulder when he probed a finger
into her soft, warm nest. She was wet. For him. Wet
and hot—how could he possibly believe it?—just for
him.

But so tight. He wasn't expecting that incredible
tightness and was suddenly afraid of hurting her, but
her palms clamped around his ears and she tugged him
down for another kiss. Her impatience made him feel

heady, strong and infinitely, primitively male. With all the past men in her life, her intense virginal tightness made no more sense than the innocence and open vulnerability in her kisses. All he could guess, all he could understand, was that past history or not, she felt differently with him.

It was easy to understand that because his whole damn world was different with her. She bucked toward him, fretful, wild, cutting off all the blood supply to his wrist and making him hurt, deep in his belly and groin. He figured his zipper was going to break, and wished it would. There was no relief or release of pressure, not this way. Every picture in his mind was of her, bare and beneath him, taking her the way he wanted to, sheathed inside her and buried deeper than any secret. Those pictures fueled his need and desire to please her. He cupped and rubbed, building heat and friction with his rough palm and finger. She said something. "Seth, I don't know how. Seth, I can't, I..."

He shushed her, not with words but with touch, looks, kisses. She didn't respond to him. She never just seemed to respond to him. She seemed to explode instead, all female fire and shimmering fireworks from the inside out. Her skin gave off a scent, a musky earthy female scent, as compelling as the magic in her trembly mouth and the dark, lost look in her eyes. She cried out, a raw, sweet sound that blended with the wind and carried over ocean and sky. Tremors shook through her, mini earthquakes that left her shuddering, and when they finally stopped, she lay there, her head buried in his shoulder in sheltering weakness.

In time, he slipped his hand free. Slowly. The spell was over, he knew, and any minute now he was going to realize what a crazy and reprehensible thing he'd done. There was no one around, but there could have been. They were openly exposed, bare to ocean and sky, and God, he didn't believe what he'd done to her. Her white throat had a red mark, and her mouth was as swollen and rosy as a bruise. Her blouse was pushed up, and her shorts bunched and tangled around her hips. She looked debauched and wasted. Thoroughly wasted. Because of him.

He smoothed and fixed and straightened, hoping she wouldn't open her eyes yet, not wanting her to realize what he'd done to her...not wanting anyone but him to see how she looked, ever. He was afraid she'd feel regrets, prayed that she felt no shame. God, he wouldn't hurt her. He'd die before hurting her.

When he finished fixing and straightening, her head tilted back in the crook of his arm. Her sleepy eyes were open, but the blinding shaft of sun made her expression hard to read. "Seth?"

"What, honey?" His whole body braced, anticipating her being upset with him. He owed her an apology for losing his head. He could think of a million powerful apologies, but no excuses. A good man, a real man—in Seth's view—had no excuses for losing all sight of emotional control anywhere near a woman.

"Seth...." She said his name again, as if it were the only word she could get past her throat for that moment. But then she sighed, and touched his cheek. "No one," she whispered, "no one, ever, made me feel so loved."

Eight

He made her feel *loved?* It was four days later, and Seth still hadn't figured out that incomprehensible statement. He'd lost his head. That was nothing for a man to feel proud of. He'd damn near taken her in full view of man, boats and sky—in full view of his dog, for cripes sake—without a single thought of protecting her or how either of them might feel afterward. If Samantha had any sense, she would have wrapped a noose around his neck and hanged him from the nearest tree. Instead Samantha had claimed in that confoundedly blissful voice that she felt *loved*.

In her eyes, he seemed to have done something right. For the life of him, Seth couldn't figure out what it was. Further, it struck him as an unfair, unreasonable and terrifying thing for a woman to do—say something like that, something that was guaranteed to gnaw on a man and worry him to death.

Distracted, he nearly bumped into a tyke wearing a bright red jacket, then had to dodge a grandmother-type juggling an armload of shopping bags. Tourists clogged the sidewalks. Instinctively he patted his back pocket, making sure the package he'd just purchased at the drug store was securely lodged out of sight. He hadn't figured on needing condoms in his budget for another decade at least. Still didn't. The purchase was stupid, embarrassing, unnecessary—and all Samantha's fault. She scared him. His whole life, he'd had good sense, good judgment, brains. Not around her. Unfortunately where he grew up, a man protected a woman and no excuses cut the mustard. The chances were a million to one that he'd let anything happen, but even with the odds that good, he was still . . . worried.

A block down, he found the shop he was looking for. Seth knew most of the stores in Bar Harbor by now, but not this one. Damned if he could explain what he was doing there, but when a man was worried sick, he didn't always do logical things. It *wasn't* his kind of place. Wind chimes tinkled when he opened the door. Herbal wreaths decorated the walls; wicker baskets of perfumy soaps and cosmetic gunk cluttered the aisles. It was one of those shops that women loved and any guy bigger than five-five risked life and limb just trying to walk through. Seth was a lot bigger than five-five.

He tucked in his elbows, found the tea section and carted his purchase to the counter fast. The clerk—and probably the owner—was wearing something that looked like a burlap blouse, a long gauzy skirt and sandals. Her earrings were like yin-yang symbols and dangled all the way to her shoulders. Seth figured Samantha'd love her. He looked over his shoulder as he dug out his wallet. "This isn't for me," he told the clerk. "I just have a friend who likes to drink ginseng tea."

"A lot of people think it's a wonderful tonic," she said peaceably.

"Yeah. That's exactly what she wants it for. A tonic." He added firmly, "*Nothing* else."

"To each his own," she murmured as she made change. "Is there anything else I can help you with?"

Now there was a question from hell, Seth thought gloomily as he drove home. No one could help him. The emotional mess he'd created was entirely his own doing. His tumbling off the deep end was understandable. Hell, no man with a heart could resist Samantha. But he'd never intended for her to care about *him*.

Since that afternoon in Acadia, nothing was the same. If it wasn't love in her eyes, it was perilously, dangerously near the mark. She seemed to assume that the natural result of the intimacies they'd shared was an increased closeness. And it was. He knew exactly what a fraud Samantha was now. She was a hopeless sucker for dogs and kids. She belonged driving that station wagon she was running from. True, she was never going to be the kind to have dinner on the table at the dot of six. Seth figured the guy who married her had better adjust early on to an insane household— and probably his suburban lawn dug up in a ragtag herb garden. But Samantha was never the free spirit she'd led him to believe. She wasn't running away from commitment or permanence or responsibility. She was just scared of hooking up with the wrong guy.

Seth knew exactly why she was attracted to him. He didn't give a flying patoot about her money or her family connections. That was a big deal to her, which he understood, but there had to be a million men on the planet with more character than the jerks she'd run into before. And none of those million would have his problem.

When he turned a corner, the sun shone straight into his eyes. He pushed down the visor, and then absently scratched his forearm. There was a tiny itchy bump just above his wrist, possibly a mosquito bite but more likely a hive. For the past two nights his sleep had been invaded by dreams—dreams of seducing her, dreams of changing from a staid, ordinary guy into exactly the lover she wanted and needed. Dreams that turned into nightmares when he failed her in bed. If he failed with Samantha, he knew he'd have a worse problem than hives. He'd die. Or wish he had the luxury of being dead.

A few minutes later, with a broody scowl, he pulled into the driveway to his house. He braked, jammed the transmission into Park, turned the key and then just sat there. The complicated, confounded problem was that loving Ms. Samantha Adams put him in a hopeless Catch-22. She'd been hurt, specifically because the men she'd chosen had all let her down.

She had no idea that as a man, he could let her down worse than all of the others.

A flash of black made him glance up. Jezebel had spotted the truck and, tail wagging, come to greet him. Seth climbed out, trying to figure out what the pup had dangling from her mouth. Some scrap of material. Orange and whitish. Sort of striped?

Tiger striped.

"Dammit, Jezzie, bring it. Give it here, girl, give it here." Seth whipped his head around, but Samantha's car was still gone. For the past few days she'd been in and out, doing local research on ghosts. He'd encouraged her. He had yet to figure out what happened in the blue bedroom—maybe he really *had* been sleepwalking and fixed the stupid wall himself. Who knew? Who cared? But Samantha, of course, did. And the busier she was researching ghosts, the less he was exposed to the temptation of her underfoot.

At this precise instant, especially, he was thrilled that she was nowhere in sight.

"Jezebel. *Drop it.* You've been in the dirty clothes hamper again, haven't you. What did I tell you yesterday? What? I told you to stay away from her underwear, that's what." Jezebel obediently dropped the tiger-striped panties and waited, innocently panting, until Seth got close enough to bend down. The pup promptly snatched them again and head high, pranced several feet away. "This is not a game, Jezebel. If you think I'm going to chase you all over this yard, you've got another think coming. You drop those *right now.*"

She dropped them again. Seth bent down again. Jezzie, faster than a streak of lightning, took off with her prize, this time running hell-bent for leather with Seth barreling after her. He was halfway across the yard when he glimpsed the red Firebird turning into the driveway. For reasons he couldn't imagine, there was a car trailing straight behind hers. She'd brought company?

Swell.

He tackled Jezebel at the far edge of the yard. They both went down in a messy, grass-staining, boisterous heap. Jezebel immediately abandoned the tiger-striped underpants. It was a tough choice, but she'd rather play roughhouse than tease.

"Seth? What are you doing? Is something wrong?"

"Not a thing," he sang out. She was walking toward him. He had thirty seconds, max, to stand up, shovel her underpants into his back pocket and produce a smile of greeting. He managed that, even with Jezebel tugging violently on his pant leg. *"Jez,"* he said sharply, and the dog promptly obeyed as if sensing something was honestly wrong.

Something was definitely wrong, Seth thought. It was in her eyes. She looked okay, not hurt, not harmed, her burnt orange jumpsuit molding her figure in a way to disastrously affect a man's heart rate, but nothing unusual there. It was just that Samantha would probably leap right into a lion's den without an ounce of nerves—she had the tendency to find sunny options in total disasters—so Seth was worried even before he took a good look at the guy trailing behind her.

"Seth, this is Judd Lightfoot. Judd, this is the owner of the house, Seth Connor." Her eyes flashed to his, clearly trying to communicate something. Damned if he knew what it was. Unlike her, he wasn't into psychic stuff such as mind reading.

One look at the stray she'd brought home, though, and Seth felt inclined to sigh. The man was about five-four. A scrawny thing with straggly long hair, limpid brown eyes, a guru-type shirt and loose, baggy pants. He was maybe thirty, and wearing enough chains around his neck to stock a jewelry store.

"Seth…" Samantha gave him another one of those meaningful, awkward, please-don't-be-irritated-with-me looks. "I didn't want to spring unexpected company on you, but I tried to call several times and you weren't home. I wasn't sure what to do. The thing is that Judd not only reads auras, but he has a degree in paranormal research. He was leaving town tomorrow morning, so if I didn't bring him out here today there wasn't going to be another chance...."

Seth shook the guy's hand, since the little squirt offered it. Samantha rambled on, but it was all in the same vein. The guy's palm was clammy and softer than a girl's. Seth figured the degree in paranormal research was worth about as much as the tale about his only being in town today. He smelled a scam.

"Samantha, honey—"

"He's communicated directly with ghosts before, Seth. It's what he does. He gave me a whole list of the places where he's been—"

"I'm sure he did."

"Naturally I wanted to ask you first, but when I couldn't reach you on the phone I wasn't sure what to do. I didn't want to pass up this chance. Mr. Lightfoot isn't in the area very often. And I thought if I just took him up to the blue bedroom, he might—"

Seth didn't want to be rude and interrupt her, but he couldn't hold back the question forever. "Exactly how much did you charge her, Mr. Lightfoot?"

The man never had a chance to answer because Samantha cheerfully jumped in. "Only fifty dollars. And that was such a steal that I—"

Fifty bucks? The jerk had fleeced her for fifty bucks? Seth took a step toward him. He wasn't going to hurt the little runt, but physically removing him from the property was going to be a pleasure.

Possibly Samantha sensed his intention, because she suddenly slipped an arm around his waist. It stopped him cold. She'd started doing that kind of thing all the time. Hooking an arm around his waist. Squeezing a hand on his shoulder. Small gestures that made his hormones buck like a rodeo bull and short-circuited all the thought processes in his brain. Dammit, when she did stuff like that, if she asked him to walk on water, he'd have at least tried.

"He won't be here long. I just want to take him up to the blue bedroom, and see if he senses a presence here. That's okay with you, isn't it?"

Of course it wasn't okay with him. The guy was probably a thief who got women to trust him into their homes where he could case the places. But hell. Seth figured he could supervise the little squirt, make sure what he touched and what he didn't, and Samantha was so clearly excited and anxious about the whole project that he just didn't have the heart to say no.

An hour later, Mr. Lightfoot was still there and Seth's opinion of the whole project had done an abrupt one-hundred-and-eighty-degree spin-around. Samantha had gotten a bargain for her fifty bucks, he thought dryly, because entertainment this outstanding was rarely that cheap.

Mr. Lightfoot had immediately sensed a "presence" in the blue bedroom. No surprise. They were all up there except for Jezebel, who'd sniffed and nuzzled all over the guy and then, bored, loped outside for a snooze.

Seth wasn't remotely inclined to nap. He was too hard-pressed to keep from laughing. Mr. Lightfoot had carted in a basket of props from his mud-crusted Chevy. Late-afternoon sun gleamed brightly through the windows, but he'd lit a dozen candles anyway.

He'd also brought a cheap brass thing of incense and lit that, too. The room was choky and smoky with the pungent smell. At the moment he was busy tossing dried weeds—"strewing herbs"—all over the freshly varnished floor, while he chanted incantations in what he called "tongue."

Seth scratched his knee. It was a great act. The guy never even cracked a smile. Samantha, sitting yoga style on the floor next to him, had listened enthralled to the guy's whole hoaxy routine... at least until Mr. Lightfoot started talking about exorcisms.

"Wait a second. I'm really not sure about that," Samantha said hesitantly.

"It's the only way," Mr. Lightfoot intoned. "For whatever reasons the spirit is trapped here, he is going to stay unless we do something actively to remove him. You want him gone, don't you?"

"Well, yes," Samantha admitted. "But an exorcism seems kind of cruel. I don't want to hurt him or anything like that. We'd just like him to...well...move on."

"Precisely," Mr. Lightfoot agreed. "And that's exactly what we're going to do."

Seth figured he'd have to intervene then, guessing the guy was gonna hit her up for more money, but apparently exorcism was included in the cover charge. And as ridiculous as the whole thing was, he thought a handy little exorcism wasn't the worst idea in town. Nothing he'd said or done had swayed Samantha from believing in this claptrap. If she really believed this guy could get rid of their "spirit," it would put a kibosh on the whole problem.

"Hold hands," Mr. Lightfoot ordered.

Seth sure didn't mind that order. Samantha scooted closer to him, knees touching knees, her fingers lacing with his. Mr. Lightfoot didn't join them. He stood up, took out a couple of painted gourds from his bag of tricks, and started shaking them and chanting.

A breeze stirred the lacy curtains. A fretful breeze, strong enough to wisp a strand of hair on Samantha's brow. The pulse was beating hard in her wrist. He thought about renting her some horror movies. She clearly loved being scared. Since she liked old movies, he figured she'd go for one of the old Hitchcock's like *Psycho,* or maybe one of the original Frankensteins or Draculas. Either way, he'd turn the lights off. He could picture her cuddling up to him, holding hands as naturally as this, her really knowing there was nothing to be scared of but just liking the feeling. Fear had a lot in common with sex. The rush, the excitement, the zip of adrenaline had the same ingredients of a turn-on—with none of the repercussions of the real thing.

Mr. Lightfoot was still chanting. The gourds looked like baby rattles to Seth. The guy's voice was squeaky. A door slammed somewhere upstairs, probably, Seth thought, because of the sudden gust of wind. But it made Samantha dart a glance at him.

He squeezed her hand and stole her a quick wink. There was nothing really scary going on here. She had to be dreaming if she thought he'd let anything happen to her.

Mr. Lightfoot raised both his arms, chanting loudly now, demanding that the spirit permanently remove his butt from the premises. His words were fancier, but that was the general gist. Both his eyes were closed. His whole scrawny body was tense, posed in dramatic concentration, his voice rising to a squawking crescendo. . . .

When his pants fell down.

Seth blinked. And then blinked again. It definitely took away from the gravity of the ceremony to see Mr. Lightfoot's baggy trousers lying in a puddle at his ankles. He wore boxers with a tennis racket design. His knees were bonier than doorknobs, and a priest in a whorehouse couldn't look more shocked.

Seth tried, but he really couldn't help it.

He burst out laughing.

"Connor, that was *very* unkind."

"I know, I know, and I'm real sorry. But did you see the way he flew down the stairs still holding his pants? I'll bet he's past the Maine border by now. I figure we're lucky he remembered his car."

Samantha's lips twitched, then firmed. "He was frightened. He really seemed to believe that it was a ghost who pulled down his pants. You shouldn't have laughed."

"Ah . . . Samantha? You were laughing as hard as I was."

"But that was your fault. I didn't mean to. It's like when someone in a room yawns and suddenly everybody else is yawning. When you start laughing, the sound is . . . well . . . catching."

Seth was enjoying being lectured, but the only thing catching, he thought, was her. Neither had been in the mood to work after Mr. Lightfoot had taken a powder from "the house of hell." It was too early for dinner, too early to settle into evening-type lazing around. Jezebel had provided an unexpected distraction when she wandered home from the beach, bringing Samantha a present of a dead fish. The fish had been good and dead, long *long* dead, and Jezzie had rolled in it first.

Samantha had no problem doing two things at the same time. While she lectured him, she was simultaneously lathering his dog in peach herbal shampoo. Seth took a slug of beer, and then lazily leaned back on his elbows in the shade of the porch steps. Females of all species, he thought dryly, were amazingly alike.

His "girls" were a dozen feet away on the grass. There was nothing hard about giving Jezebel a bath; she loved anything to do with water, but it was definitely her first experience with peach herbal shampoo. She was sitting as still as a goddess, sudsed from neck to tail, her eyes closed in near ecstasy.

Seth considered saving Samantha, then changed his mind. She'd not only volunteered for the bath detail, but she had the hose—which should have indicated who was in control. Of course, it wasn't quite working out that way. Samantha was already covered in more peach lather than the pup, with suds and damp spots clinging to her rayon jumpsuit, and where Jezzie was more than willing to sit for the washing part, his dog was savvy about hoses. They were good for drinks. They were good for carrying around and making humans swear at you. And they were *really* great for getting humans all wet.

"Seth, seriously, maybe it *was* the ghost who made his pants fall down."

"And maybe the guy needs to wear a belt," Seth said wryly.

"Maybe Jock—" Samantha, attempting to curtail Jezzie's exuberant enthusiasm, was fast running out of breath "—didn't want to be exorcised."

"Hell, if I were a self-respecting ghost, I wouldn't want that little pip-squeak exorcising me, either."

"He wasn't a pip-squeak. He had all kinds of credentials, not just a degree in paranormal behavior, but—Seth, quit laughing."

"I'm not laughing at him. I figure a guy who has tennis rackets on his boxer shorts deserves all the sympathy he can get. It's you I'm laughing at, Adams."

"Me?" The hose twisted like a snake, abetted by Jezzie. A squish of water squirted straight into her face, making her gasp and choke. "You *could* help me!"

Not true. At that instant he was incapable of doing anything but plopping down his beer and holding his stomach. It'd be nothing to give Jezzie a bath, she'd said. Her hair was hanging in soggy clumps. Her bare feet were muddy and grassy. Jezzie loved her, and Jezzie chose that moment for a cuddle. Samantha went down in a wet heap, directly on her fanny, while Jezebel tried to earnestly and lavishly thank her for the bath.

"Connor!"

"I'll help. I'll help." His belly hurt from laughing so hard, and tears were starting to spring from his eyes. He took a big gulp of air to control himself, then glanced at her again. A mistake. A big mistake. He'd just never seen her looking anything but truly beautiful, a man's fantasy of temptation and desire and sultry beauty, and right now, he wasn't sure a cat would drag her home. "I'm coming. I really am. I just need a second..."

He meant the ardent promises; it's just that they came out in gasps and guffaws. He opened his mouth to say something apologetic and conciliatory—stuff he honestly *meant*—but he never got it out before a splat of water hit him full in the face. When his vision cleared, he got another one. The hose water was spring-fed cold, about fifty degrees of straight frigid shock, and Samantha—did the woman have no mercy?—was holding her thumb on the nozzle to direct it just right.

Holding his hand to deflect the spray from his face, he aimed for her.

"Jezzie, do you think big ol' Seth needs a bath? *I* think he needs a bath. I think a bath is just what the doctor ordered for his sick, sick, sick sense of humor.... Now, Seth. Now, *Seth*. Be nice. It was just a joke. Don't you dare. Don't you *dare*—"

He chased her halfway across the yard and captured the hose, but Jezebel stole it back. The tug-of-war ended up with shrieks and screams and rainbow arches of water caught in the pale buttery sunlight. By the time he collapsed in the grass, he was soaked through, freezing, and panting harder than his worn-out puppy.

Samantha crashed next to him. She was so whipped she could hardly catch a breath, but Sam being Sam, she had to gloat. "I guess I taught *you* a lesson," she said.

"I guess you did."

He turned his head to look at her. It hit him slow and hard like a slow-motion bullet in a dark alley, nothing he was expecting or prepared for. Her feet were muddy, her clothes a disaster, her chest heaving and her hair a witch's wet tangle and he was hopelessly in love with her.

It wasn't news, that he was falling for her. But Seth had been trying to think of it as if it were an affliction—something he'd get over, like a bad case of flu. Something he could control, if he just tried hard enough. She was never supposed to become a critical part of his life.

The stab in his chest felt as painfully tight as the squeeze of a vise. Too easily—too *damn* easily—he could imagine waking up with her in the morning, coming home to her after work, a couple of kids with her Cleopatra eyes and sassy smiles running all over him. She was always going to attract shysters like Lightfoot. It would be part of his job as her husband, saving her from predators, and part of his job to build her confidence that nobody and no one would ever hurt her when he was around. Only it was stupid—unforgivably stupid to let himself think anything along those lines.

She was looking at him now, with laughter in her eyes. Laughter, love and the dance of teasing that Seth knew damn well was an invitation. It would be so easy to sweep her into his arms, kiss her senseless, kiss her witless, give in to the sensual tension that had been driving them both nuts. Easy—if it hadn't been for Gail.

He kept forgetting Gail when he was with Samantha, couldn't seem to think about other women, any other women, which was a dangerous error in judgment. He'd wilted when it counted. That wasn't something a man could forget, nothing any man could forget. And to risk the humiliation of failure with Samantha—to be less than the man she needed and wanted—was a risk, pure and simple, that he was too damned terrified to take.

"Hey..." Samantha twisted around to a sitting position. "A second ago, you were laughing. Suddenly you look so serious. What's wrong?"

"Nothing. I was just thinking that you'd better get in the house and into a hot shower before you catch pneumonia."

"Seth...?"

She heard the sudden harshness in his voice, and he saw the flash of hurt in her eyes. It couldn't be helped. He lurched to his feet, needing to put distance between them for her sake as well as his. "You're starting to shiver. Up and at 'em, lady. I'll race you to the house."

Nine

Samantha had been chilled when she first ran upstairs, but that was more than an hour ago. Submerged to the neck in the old-fashioned, claw-footed bathtub, she broodily flipped on more hot water—as if she weren't already as wrinkled as a prune and hot enough to bake.

Moisture dribbled down the marble sink. The walls and checkerboard tile floor were coated with steam. Outside, the sun was dropping fast. She hadn't turned on a light, and the lone north window only let in murky shadows. Between the dusk and the swirls of steamy mist, she could barely see. It didn't matter. The murky gloom suited her mood.

The foggy steam was so thick that she never saw the doorknob suddenly turn—but she heard the clicky squeak. There was no chance to reach for a towel before a big black head appeared through the doorway.

She let out a sigh. "Not now, Jezebel. Out. Scoot.
Trust me, I'm not fit company for man or beast right
now, and you'll swelter in here with the heat."

Apparently the dog didn't care. She lumbered in,
sniffed at the coconut bath salts, and promptly
flopped on the rag rug with a lazy dog sigh—leaving a
giant draft of cold air still gusting from the open
doorway. Exasperated, Samantha climbed from the
tub, jogged dripping across the room, closed the door
and then hustled back into the tub with a baleful
glance at Jezzie.

The dog had become hopelessly, endearingly attached to her. But Samantha was coming to the unal-
terable conclusion that Jezzie's owner was never going
to suffer that same attachment.

Nothing monumental had happened. Seth had just
done it again. Shut her off at the pass. Their crazy
water fight outside had been nothing but fun—until
that moment when they'd been lying together in the
grass. The most casual touch ignited desire in his eyes.
The most innocent smile could catch the same spark.
But there came a point, every time, when he seemed to
realize how close they were becoming. And just like
those other times, he suddenly turned tense and
tight—and took off faster than a bat out of hell.

Samantha pressed a washcloth over her eyes. Seth
was too kind to outright reject her, but—wasn't it time
she faced it?—the rare, powerful, compelling emotions between them were all on one side. Her side.
Only hounds bayed at the moon. She'd been kidding
herself that he needed her. Maybe she'd been kidding
herself that he even, ever, wanted her—

"Lar, you're a beauty, lass."

At the sound of the guttural masculine voice, Samantha dropped the washcloth. The whole room was dusk and steam, but there was no sudden change, no sound, no door opening or movement. Jezebel didn't even stir from the rag rug on the tile floor.

"I didna appreciate your bringing in that lad. All that tomfoolery and incantation nonsense truly offended me, but I suppose I forgive ye, lass. It gave me an easy chance to make the two of ye laugh, did it not, when his trousers fell down? So I didna really mind."

Instinctively Samantha pulled up her knees and wrapped her arms around them. Not *now,* she thought impatiently. It wasn't the first time she'd heard the voice of her seventeenth-century pirate. She'd never denied that Jock existed. She'd always wanted to believe in him. But right now she felt fragile because of Seth—fragile, vulnerable and as unsteady as a leaf in a high wind. She just had no time or patience for this nonsense.

"... The two of you are starting to make my existence a hell. An ol' pirate like me, ye'd think I knew nothing of love. But I do, lass. 'Twas the only thing I ever did right in my life. I willna burn yer tender ears with tales of my experience with women, but ye've surely heard of Teach. Edward Teach. They called him Blackbeard in my day. He thought himself the better lover but 'twas never true. I was far more skilled. *Far* more. But there now, I dona want to digress from the point at hand...."

Any minute now, Samantha figured, she was going to get a grip. The only time she was susceptible to hearing Jock was when she was grappling with her feelings for Seth. Which meant that the only logical conclusion she could reach was that he was a product of her own mind. Which was fine. It just felt so...silly. Imagining voices by moonlight and fog was one thing—but not while a dog was snoozing and a phone was ringing downstairs and everything was everyday natural and normal.

"...Ye two are as stubborn as goats. Ye're in love with him, lassie, and he's even more crazy for you. I do na comprehend why either of you are making this so hard. Seth's the one trying my patience, he is. He looks at you like ye're the sun and the moon, and he walks around with a saber edge to his mood. 'Tisna difficult to figure out that he's near dying from frustration, and I canna understand why the lad does not make the obvious move and seduce ye...ah, sweetling, now I've gone and scared ye, have I?"

Samantha had no idea if she was scared or not, but her heart was suddenly racing and her skin covered with goose bumps. Quietly and carefully, her toe flipped the drain. Cautiously slow, she reached for a towel. Tomorrow, undoubtedly, it would strike her as humorously ironic that a ghost was trying to counsel her on true love, when the man she loved was haunted by ghosts. Just now, though, it didn't strike her as funny. Real or not real, Jock was treading on intimately private fears and feelings that were too damn close to home, and she wanted out of there.

"Ahh, lassie, you have a figure out of a man's dream...."

She wrapped the towel around her, tight and fast.

"...A fine plump fanny. Beautiful—"

"*Jezebel,* wake up. Come with me. *Come,* girl—"

"...Do na lose patience with him, sweetling. Do na lose faith. I'm telling ye true—he needs ye. It just takes

a spot of time for certain men to come around. I'll
help ye. In truth, I have an idea or two—''

Advice and ideas from a dirty-minded voyeur of a
ghost with a soft spot for love? She'd certify herself
before listening any further. Yanking open the door,
she streaked down the hall with her towel flapping. In
seconds, she had the door closed on the gold bedroom next to Seth's, and then—impatiently—had to
open it again. Jezebel lumbered in. Once the dog was
safely inside, Samantha not only closed the door, but
locked it.

She'd been sleeping in the bedroom for weeks now.
Sometime, a hundred years ago, it must have been a
woman's sitting room. The gold brocade chaise, the
standing mirror and marble dressing stand, the chest
of cabled wood and fringed lamp shade were all feminine trappings. Samantha had loved it on sight, but
now she leaned against the stucco wall, staring at the
furnishings without seeing anything.

She'd always been open-minded. Always. Who
knew if some of the UFO citings were real? How could
any human be so arrogant as to think the human species were the only sentient beings in the universe?
Premonitions and déjà vu and sixth senses and spirits—she'd always been drawn and attracted to believing in all of those as well. There *was* magic in life. As
a woman she'd always known that it was the things in
life that you couldn't see or touch that mattered most.
Loyalty, honor, truth. Love.

Samantha pushed a strand of damp hair from her
brow. The ghost hadn't shaken her. It was hearing her
own feelings expressed, her own hopes about Seth
wanting her, needing her, and yeah, loving her.

What she wanted to believe and what was reality were too different things. That was old news. She'd made mistakes in judgment about men before. She'd also violently sworn that she would never again make the mistake of falling for a man who didn't want her.

Maybe she was hard to love. Add some Adams influence and money and men had always come flocking, but never for her, never just for herself. Maybe her specific personality flaws made loving her just too impossible. She was a tad flaky. A teensy bit stubborn, some might even say bullheaded. Once Samantha started cataloging her flaws, she could come up with several thousand...but none that had seemed so insurmountable before. There hadn't been anyone, not before, whom she *wanted* to love her. No one had ever mattered like Seth. No one had ever...

"Samantha?" Seth's voice thundered from the bottom of the stairs. "I heard you running up there. Is anything wrong?"

"I was just hustling out of a bath. Everything's fine," she called back. The fib came out as bright and sharp as pride. She'd coaxed her company on Seth; she'd been natural and honest with him, and she'd expressed her willingness to deepen the relationship as flagrantly as her pride would allow. If he didn't feel the same, then he didn't. If Samantha had learned anything painfully and indelibly from life, it was that you couldn't force love.

She understood about the ghosts in his life. She understood that a Jezebel-type had hurt him, but if he wasn't willing to open the door, she had absolutely no way to get through to the other side.

It was time, she thought, that she went home.

* * *

Something, Seth thought, was disastrously wrong. He couldn't imagine what had happened from the time she ran upstairs until now, but something clearly had.

She wasn't eating. Everyone had ups and downs in appetite. But not her. He was tempted to check the yellow pages for the address of the nearest emergency room. Nothing put Samantha off her food.

Neither of them had wandered into the kitchen until past dusk. She'd put together sub sandwiches on thick slices of French bread, slathering hers with hot sauce. A bowl of mounded grapes sat on the kitchen table, so did a fresh baked batch of brownies, some leftover strawberry cheesecake, a plate of pickles and another of potato chips. The combination was enough to turn the average stomach. Not hers. She was crazy for grapes. Hell, she was crazy for all of it. She'd normally dive into the pickles and cheesecake in alternate bites and be adding extra hot sauce to her sandwich.

Instead she was taking occasional ladylike nibbles. And not many of those.

"Are you still thinking about that Lightfoot guy?" he asked her. About the last thing on earth he wanted to bring up was ghosts, but she was starting to scare him with those ladylike nibbles. Whatever was bugging her, he wanted out in the open.

"Lightfoot? No. I'd forgotten all about him. Have some brownies, Seth."

She passed him the cheesecake, not the brownies, then rambled on about a movie title she was trying to remember. An old one, a classic with Bogart and Hepburn. They were on a boat. It was set in Africa. War time. None of that rang a bell for Seth until she mentioned a scene with leeches.

"African Queen," he supplied.

"Oh, thank heavens. Trying to remember that would have driven me crazy all night."

Her fetish for old films was typical, so was her ditsiness at passing him the wrong dish. Seth pushed the hot sauce closer to her, thinking it might spur her to eat. It didn't.

She looked fine. No sign of fever. She'd come downstairs wearing some kind of loose silky pants and a voluminous coral shirt. Not fancy by her standards, just the kind of thing she liked to lounge around in on a quiet evening. No makeup, no earrings, her feet were bare and her hair was tucked behind her ears. The artificial light made her face look pale, though. She kept flashing him smiles, but they were all low voltage. And her usual high-wire energy level was strangely missing.

"You tired?" he asked her.

"No. Just fine. How about you?"

"Doing great, except for feeling full to the brim."

"Me, too." She started to gather up the dishes. He watched her put the cheesecake on the counter and the brownies in the fridge.

The flu? The curse? He trailed after her, taking care of the cheesecake, filling the sink with soapy water, trying to think of something that would pep her up. "If you're not too beat, maybe it'd be a good night to explore the lighthouse," he suggested.

"It's dark."

"So we'll take flashlights."

"It's still locked up, isn't it?"

"I'll find the key."

"Don't you think it's turned a little chilly?"

Her token objections were bewildering, since the last
he knew, she was dying to explore the lighthouse.
Eventually, though, he talked her into it, and went
looking for the antiquated key while she went upstairs to fetch her jacket. She came back downstairs a
couple minutes later. She'd put on shoes—a pair of
soft-soled tennies—but she seemed to have forgotten
all about the coat. He didn't say anything, just tossed
her his leather jacket and yanked on a sweatshirt for
himself.

His jacket fit her twice over, but she stuck her hands
into the pockets and they ambled outside. It was cool
but not cold, the spicy ocean air scenting one of the
rare nights where the air was clearer than crystals. She
fell in step beside him, quiet, not talking, and not
looking where she was going, either—he grabbed her
arm when she nearly barreled straight into a rock. An
alarm clock kept buzzing in his mind. Everyone had
periods of moody blues. She was entitled. It was just
that she was usually an incurable optimist, a magic
believer, inclined to see the bright side of black in
everything in life.

It was probably the curse, he told himself. PMS.
Something like that. He wouldn't ask her or do anything embarrassing like that; he'd just be quiet and
understanding and make sure she didn't walk into any
more rocks, and maybe by the time they got home, he
could get her to eat something.

The white lighthouse loomed, tall, standing on a
grassy, weedy knoll on a pinnacle of land. Naturally
all the new lighthouses were automatic, but this one
was built in the old, old days, when the keeper lived in
an attached house and the beacon light had to be
handled manually. Breakers crashed and splashed on

the shore. The moon wasn't quite full, more like three-quarters, but it cast enough silvery light to make the flashlight unnecessary until they reached the door.

He dug in his jeans pocket for the key, and was thankful for the darkness because he suddenly flushed. His fingers connected with the metal key, but also with a couple of unexpected textures, something whispery soft and something crinkly. Her tiger-striped panties and the condoms. At that precise moment, he didn't want to be reminded of either.

Head bent, he concentrated on opening the door. No small task. The key fit the lock, but it didn't want to turn. Heaven knew how many years it had been since anyone had explored the old thing, and the lock was crusted with rust. He had to jerk hard before it finally gave. The round plank door creaked open, loud enough to send an uneasy frisson down his spine.

"Wow," Samantha murmured. "What a fantastic atmosphere."

Finally a sign of life from her. He should have guessed it would take something spooky... and the inside definitely qualified for the label. He shot the flashlight up and around. The light caught in the long, lacy spin of intricate spiderwebs. A rust-caked ax hung from a hook on the wall. The whole space smelled dusty and closed up. There were no windows at ground level, and nothing else to see except for a winding set of circular metal stairs leading up. At some point, there'd been a wooden railing, but it had rotted through in places.

"Let me go first. There's no telling what shape the stairs are in."

"Which means that I should go first," Samantha said logically. "If I fell through a stair and got hurt, you could carry me out. But if you crashed through, I'd be up a creek without a paddle, no way to help you."

"If I thought you could get hurt, we wouldn't be here at all." That was so obvious to Seth that it wasn't worth saying, but he let her climb ahead of him. Her footstep was light on the stairs, but the sound still echoed in the closed, round chamber. They climbed the equivalent of three stories, his flanking right behind her, until they reached a postage-stamp size landing and another rough plank door.

"It's locked," she announced.

"It better not be. I only know about the one key." But it wasn't locked. The door was just stuck from years of disuse, and when he pushed his shoulder against it hard, it sprang open.

"Heavens," she breathed.

Seth wasn't into magic the way she was, but he had to admit it was one hell of a view. They could see forever. Windows circled the room, the glass reflecting the ebony sky and diamond-tipped ocean and lights shimmering and dancing in the harbor miles away. The waves splashing below looked uncontrollably wild from here, making the lighthouse seem like a separate, isolated miniworld with no link to anything civilized.

"Can't you picture it? The sounds of foghorns and a lashing rain...the lighthouse keeper struggling to keep the beacon lit, soaked through, a clipper ship crashing through the storm, off course, headed straight for the rocks unless he can save it...."

Amused, Seth smiled. Her imagination was firing on all pistons again. She was definitely feeling better, he thought. "You think that's how it was?"

"Yes. Don't you?" She never turned to face him, never skipped a breath. "Seth, I need to tell you something. Actually I need to tell you two things. Preferably both at the same time. And real quick, okay?"

"Okay." Seth anticipated her spinning another romantic story, probably one involving Errol Flynn and pirates and storms.

She said, "I'm in love with you." And then, "I'm leaving."

Maybe pairing those two announcements made sense to her. He felt as if someone had hit him in the pit of his stomach with a blow torch. She hadn't even turned her head. In fact, her gaze was riveted on the view as if nothing else were on her mind.

"I thought about not saying anything. About loving you. I mean, I know when anyone says something like that, the other person feels put on the spot to say something back. And I don't want you to feel uncomfortable. I just wanted to tell you, because you're impossibly lovable, Connor, and I really wasn't sure if you knew that. For the record, it was nothing you did, nothing you could have helped. How could you possibly help being special? But I don't think you realize that you're special, either. I have no idea who made you feel ordinary, or where you even got that whole stupid idea, but *someone* has to tell you that you're wrong, and if I'd just gone home without ever saying a word—"

"Samantha, you're talking so fast that I can't catch up. Could you stop for a second? Just for a second?"

"Sure," she said.

But damned if he knew what to do or say then. He turned her to face him. She willingly tilted her head.

She'd said "sure" with typical Samantha-type sass; her lips were even curved in a typical Samantha-type smile. But the pulse was thudding hard in her throat. She'd tossed out her feelings of love lightly, brightly, as if reassuring him that she fully, completely understood those feelings weren't returned.

"I was afraid I'd make you feel awkward. I'm sorry."

The light was shivery, silvery in her eyes. Fragile eyes. Vulnerable eyes, as black as moonshine and midnight with just that hint of quicksilver. She didn't know, Seth thought. She had no idea how he felt about her. She'd run into too many men who wanted to use her, he knew that, but never guessed how that would affect her perception. She really had no understanding of how beautiful she was. How beautiful, how impossibly confusing, how breathtakingly desirable, how aggravatingly idealistic, how hopelessly sunshiny, how... lovable. Soul-heart-body-mind lovable.

He couldn't stand there forever. He had to say something. It just took a minute before he could get any words past the lump of sand in his throat. "You're leaving? Because of me?"

"Yes. For once I'm being realistic—a drastic change of pace for me, wouldn't you agree?" She offered him a fleeting smile. "But I'm not trying to be funny, Seth, just honest. I'm afraid I'm just going to make it more awkward for you, the longer I'm around. Why fib about it or beat around the bush? I'm not dying. My heart isn't broken. But I can't seem to shut off how I feel, and I've never been good about hiding my emotions—"

"You're terrible," he agreed, and kissed her.

"Seth?"

"What?"

"You don't have to kiss me—"

The hell he didn't.

"You don't want this—"

She had that dead wrong, too.

"Connor, you're totally confusing me. The whole reason that I...look, I *know* you don't want things to get sticky—"

Seth knew exactly, precisely, the mountain-huge reason why he didn't want things to get sticky. Only this was about her, not him. It had nothing to do with his terror of wilting. It had to do with her, feeling unwanted, feeling unloved, feeling—stupid, Samantha was so damned stupid—that no guy was going to love her separate from her Adams pedigree.

When he took her mouth, her lips met his and clung. Tongues tangled and tasted. She made a sound, a raw sweet yearning sound, and the moonlight played on her face, on the sweep of eyelashes on her cheeks, on her pearl-white skin, on her mouth, wet and parted, hungry for his.

Her responsiveness had always driven him crazy. Before, that was something he'd tried to hide. Now, it was something he wanted her to know. He didn't give a damn where she came from, never had, never would. It was always just her. When he was with her, when he was touching her, he wasn't ordinary; he wasn't plain old Seth, an average guy on the street. He was a hundred feet tall, an epic lover, infused and suffused with masculine power because that's how she made him feel.

His hand cupped her nape, then glided down the slope of her shoulders. The slightest push and his

oversized leather jacket slipped easily off her. It fell to
the floor with a plop and whoosh, the only sound in
the lighthouse chamber except for her breathing, and
his. Freed of the constraint, her hands climbed up his
chest and then wound tight, tight around his neck.

His heart started skipping beats, like an engine
flooding from too rich fuel. He wanted her to feel de-
sired, wanted, loved. He wanted her to know that he'd
always found her precious, unforgettable, infinitely
special. He'd never held back those feelings because of
anything wrong with her. Only proving that to her,
showing her, meant kissing her the way he really felt.
Touching her the way he'd wanted to for weeks.

And Samantha seemed to be getting the message.
Only too well. She'd never had a bank vault of inhi-
bitions, but hell, he'd never planned on unleashing a
tidal wave. Her mouth was soft, softer than pussy
willows and rose petals, but she returned each kiss with
a powder keg of pressure and yearning. She leaned
into his body with open vulnerability, her tummy
grazing his hard abdomen, her thighs molding against
his. Her movements were a thousand times more sensuous than seductive. It wasn't as if she were thinking
about it. It was just as if she knew, she'd always
seemed to know, exactly what stirred his blood.

He needed air. Quick, real quick. But when he tried
to lift his head, she framed his face and tugged him
down again. Down to her. Kiss followed kiss, each
deeper and intimately darker than the last. She
matched stroke for stroke, caress for caress, until he
lost all sense of who was touching who. She pushed up
his sweatshirt. Somehow it ended up over his head,
hurled somewhere. Somehow her coral blouse got unbuttoned, skimmed off her shoulders and down her

arms. The blouse was silky, but not half as silky as the texture of her skin. He pinched the single hook, and then her scrap of bra was gone, too.

He lifted her, his hands cupping her fanny, so he could nuzzle the sweet flesh between her breasts. She arched her spine on a fretful groan. He powdered more kisses on her ivory skin, wishing he'd seen her bare before, exalting because she was bare for him now. The tips of her breasts were hard, tight, tender. There was a flash of moonlight, then shadow, when he dipped back down. He could have found her, blind, in a crowd of a million women, solely by her scent, by her response, by how impossibly incredible she made him feel.

His belt buckle was digging into her tender flesh. He didn't know until she murmured his name. "Seth." Until she said it like an aching, wooing plea. He felt her hand reach down to his belt, find the buckle, hesitate. She was asking if she could open it. Her eyes asked him, velvet-black eyes, her gaze suddenly searching his face with a shyness and fear that he'd never seen before, not in her.

That was the moment, the only moment, when he could have stopped the whole thing. He hadn't totally lost control. Not then, not yet. He still knew where they were. The whole place was impossible and wrong, chilly, dusty, no bed, no place to even sit much less lie with her. Yet that didn't stop him.

The risk of failing her should have. That fear seized him, filled him with a sinking-lead sensation. If he let things go even an inch further, it was all going down. He'd risk humiliating himself, risk failing the woman he loved as a lover. Only he'd never planned, never anticipated, anything mattering more than that risk of failure. And she did. If the absolute worst happened, at least Samantha would know that the problem was him, not her. He had no other way to show her that he'd never kept a distance by choice, or because he didn't care, or because there was anything wrong with her. She'd always been perfect. Perfect for him, perfect to him. She was magic, fire, life. He was damnably afraid that she'd captured a corner of his soul, a corner he'd never get back if he lost her.

"You're going to have to say no pretty quick, Seth, if you don't want this," she whispered.

He was pretty sure that was supposed to be the man's line. Then, with her eyes glued on his face, she flipped the belt buckle. The sound, in the sudden dark stillness, made his blood rush with the heat of a lightning streak. "You're the one who has the choice," he said hoarsely.

"You're my choice."

She said it so simply that he damn near lost it then. But he needed to tell her. "I have protection."

"Thank heavens one of us is prepared. I didn't know this was going to happen. I was so positive that you didn't want me."

He caught the palest hint of a tremor in her voice. And hated it. He had no choice but to reach for the truth and offer it to her. "I always wanted you. I want you now, like an unbearable clawing inside me. You've made me crazy from the day I met you."

"Good."

"That's *not* good."

"I think it's wonderful. And I think, I'm wondering, if I could make you feel any crazier. If that would be okay?"

As if she needed to ask permission. Seth took the problem of the belt away from her, loosened the catch, then the button, then freezed the zipper on his jeans. He burst free, vulnerably exposing exactly how swollen and hot he was for her. *Don't fail her,* growled through his head. And he tried to concentrate on that fear. He tried to worry about it. Only he just couldn't seem to keep his mind on himself.

She slipped off her pants, down off her hips, down to her ankles where she could step out of them. That left her only wearing panties. They were nothing, a scarlet siren red scrap of silk, a teensy ribbon of lace holding them up at the hips, nothing that even tried to cover her and so, so typical of Sam. She was a vision of moonlit-white skin and sleek long limbs, her breasts bare and full and tilted toward him. Sassy. She was so sassy that she'd scare any man who didn't have a full quota of masculine ego, and God, that look in her eyes. *You're mine, Seth Connor, and I'm gonna have you.*

He jerked out of his jeans, but he was determined to snare enough sanity to at least make them a bed. His jacket and sweatshirt wouldn't make much of a mattress, yet they were at least something to shield her, protect her. Only he'd barely crouched down before she crouched down, too, facing him, her arms reaching for him and her eyes asking to be held, as if even a second's separation was too much to be borne.

With one hand blind he groped for the jacket, but his other arm went around her and his mouth found hers. And then he forgot about fixing a bed. He forgot about everything, because she was winding her arms around him and taking him down.

He'd never been in waters this deep. There was a drumming in his ears that blocked out all sound. From the beginning he'd so ruefully known that she was a fantasy, his fantasy, the way every man dreamed of being seduced by a Lorelei, a woman so tempting he couldn't resist, a woman so sensuous and sensual that she exulted in sex and uniquely responded to him as a man.

He'd been so wrong. The reality of Samantha was a thousand times more potent than any fantasy. Nothing came easy, nothing went smooth. It was as if every fear and insecurity she ever had was painfully exposed, and he had the chance to be there for her. It was elbows bumping, and him struggling to find the damned condom, and laughing with her instead of being embarrassed. Even in the middle of that low, secret laughter, though, there was a fire building, stroking and lapping at them both. He had the feeling of being pulled into the whoosh and whirr of the blades of a fan, spinning into the binding, bonding web of intimacy. Needs were going down. Needs that dived deep, deep, into revealing waters where he didn't have a prayer of hiding anything from her, where the honesty between them was raw, desperate, sweet. Her skin was as wet as his, her breath coming just as rough and patchy, her eyes luminous and as wide open as his own.

They could have been in a sultan's palace instead of an old, dusty plank floor with naked moonlight spilling down on them. It wouldn't have made any difference. Nothing made any difference but her. She wanted him. She needed him, and she showed him her heart with every look, every touch. He could be anything with her. Anyone he wanted to be.

The only thing on earth he wanted to be was her lover.

Taking her was the only thought in his head. When he knelt over her, he was aware of how instinctively she wrapped her legs around him, aware of the frustration driving them both, aware of her musky scent and her swollen mouth and her nails biting into his shoulders. Maybe the fear of wilting should have reoccurred to him then, and maybe it would have, if he had any memory of failing, any memory of being with any other woman. But there was no one but the two of them. There was only Samantha, and every feeling and emotion she aroused was a first for him.

He never anticipated, though, that he was arousing some firsts for her. When he slid into her warmth, the only instinct driving him was release, for him, for her, and the hell of a delicious climb it was going to take them both to get there. He expected her tightness, knew her body well enough to know exactly how small she was built. And there was no barrier, no physical wall or outright clue that she was a virgin. He'd never slept with a virgin, so possibly he wouldn't have known for positive even with those clues.

But it was in her eyes. It was in her sudden startled cry, not pain, but real discomfort, and at a moment when he'd have killed himself, happily and several times over, before hurting her in any possible way.

He was mad at her for not telling him. But not then. Right then he seemed to have unleashed a lioness, and she was in no mood for chitchat. It was like getting between Samantha and her food. Not a good idea. When Samantha felt loved, by God, there was just no stopping her. She wanted her pleasure, and she wanted it now. She wanted *him*. And damned if he had a prayer of denying her anything she wanted, not then, maybe not ever, not as long as it was within his power to give her.

He loved her.

At that precise moment, nothing else could possibly matter but that.

Ten

His bed, Samantha had to admit, was infinitely more comfortable than the floor in the lighthouse. Not that she cared. She would have been content lying naked in an Arctic tundra—as long as she was wrapped in Seth's arms.

Moonlight winked through the French doors, splaying on an antique zebra-wood chiffonier and the deep scarlet hues of a Persian rug. It was late, long past midnight. Jezebel lay near the door, a bedraggled white stuffed animal tucked between her paws, her snores the only sound in the silent house.

Samantha snuggled closer in the curve of Seth's shoulder, musing how differently the night had gone than she'd expected. By now she assumed she'd be on the road—driving out of his life—never that she'd end up in his bed. Making love had been another shock. Every woman had preconceptions about the first time.

She'd anticipated awkwardness, pain, embarrassment. Seth had blown that myth right out of the water.

Afterward could have been a mountain of awkwardness, too, and instead the last half hour had been a blur of shared intimacy and rich laughter. They'd run home, half-dressed, carrying clothes, hustling and laughing because their bare feet were so cold in the dewy wet grass. Both had pelted upstairs, Jezebel bounding at their heels. At the top of the dark hallway, she'd hesitated, nervously uncertain what to do, but Seth had steered her automatically, easily, to his bedroom. There seemed no question in his mind where she would sleep, where he wanted her to be.

Her lips curved in a sleepy smile, recalling how he'd ordered her under the covers before she froze to death. She'd crawled into the pedestal bed. Once he stripped down, he climbed in, too, heaped covers over both of them...and then yelped. She *was* chilled, her feet and hands freezing and her fanny—he claimed teasingly—as shockingly cold as an iceberg. She'd tried to move away, but Seth wasn't buying that sale. He'd scooped her into the nest of his body, trapped her hands against the warmth of his chest and rubbed her down without mercy.

If she'd been happier, she couldn't remember when. Everything with Seth came honestly, naturally, with an aching sweet feeling of rightness. She was toast warm now, thanks to her merciless masseur. His brisk rubbing had gradually turned into desultory, sensual caresses, a like-to-touch and a need-to-hold communicated without his needing to say a thing.

He was falling asleep, she thought. Eventually she would, but she didn't want to. Not yet. She'd discovered wonder this night. Wonder with him, and snuggled so close in his arms, his bareness aroused the soft, secret buzz of desire. It was a gentle buzz, not a need to make love again—he'd sated her completely—but the mystery of feeling loved by him was still new. She wanted to savor it, this bone-liquid feeling of belonging to him.

"Samantha . . . you should have told me."

She tilted her head. He'd been so still that she'd never guessed he was still awake. "Told you what?" she murmured.

"You know what. That you were a virgin."

"Oh. That." She cuddled back in the curve of his shoulder. "Actually I thought I lost my virginity around the time I was five."

"You *what?*"

She chuckled in the darkness. "I played a lot of doctor. It was my favorite game. Used to round up all the boys in the neighborhood—at least until one of the mothers caught on to me. What a hoopla. I was grounded for moral corruption before I even started kindergarten. I'm not shocking you, am I? I'm pretty sure you already knew I had extensive experience with boys."

"I don't give a damn what you did with boys, Ms. Adams. I thought you had extensive experience with men."

"I have."

"Horseradish, you have."

She shifted up on an elbow. He sounded teasing, but she wasn't sure. The moonlight didn't stretch to the bed. She could see his eyes, as dark as a deep pool of tears, but the lurking shadows made it impossible to read his expression. "Connor, I've been around more blocks than I can count. The first time I fell head over heels I was sixteen. The only reason he asked me out was so his family could have an in with mine—his dad wanted my mother to fix some confounded zoning regulation. When I found that out...well, it burned pretty deep. So the next time I was more wary, and by the time after that, being cautious was automatic. I never planned on being the last virgin alive in the '90s. I just didn't want to be used."

He heard her. The whole time he was listening, his hand sieved gently, softly through her hair. "It was a gift, Samantha. You should have told me. And I could have hurt you—physically hurt you, because of not knowing. You should have told me for that reason, too."

"You didn't hurt me. I was never worried that you would. And I wasn't sure you'd think of it like a gift. A lack of experience is embarrassing at my ancient, advanced age." She brushed her hand through his crinkly chest hair. Even if she couldn't see him clearly, she could feel his heart suddenly pounding a staccato beat under her palm. He was still holding her. The weight of his arm still felt protective, possessive, but she sensed something troubling him. There was a tension behind his questions, something her answers weren't giving him. "Seth...did you *want* me to have a lot of experience before?"

"No." He hesitated. "But it changes things."

"Changes what?" When he didn't immediately answer, she said softly, "If you're worried that I have regrets, you're out of your mind. Making love with you was the best thing that ever happened to me."

"It was the *only* thing that ever happened to you. You don't have any basis to compare."

It seemed a curious thing for him to say. "Yeah, I do," she said. "I have a hundred million men in my past. I've told you before. I have an infinitely huge basis to compare."

"Not . . . sexually."

That word didn't have to be a land mine. It was the flat, careful way he said it that made Samantha suddenly feel like a minnow floundering in touchy, troubled seas. She had the strongest intuition that they'd never been talking about her previous sexual experience—but his. And that something had happened that mattered to him, something she didn't know, a clue to Seth's feelings that she'd never guessed. "Seth . . . I know this question is prying, but could we get the ghost out of the closet? Did you break up with that Jezebel because she cheated on you?"

"Jezzie?" His thick eyebrows arched in quizzical wings.

She wasn't fooled by the humor in his expression. "Not your dog. The woman. Some woman. Come on, Connor, you know all my embarrassing secrets. You think I can't handle some of yours?"

"Honey, I'm not about to talk about another woman in your bed."

"Hell's bells, you think I care about bedside etiquette? We'll make our own. What was her name?"

"Why do I have the feeling that you're gonna hound me about this until I tell you?"

"Probably because you're a brilliant, intelligent man?"

But she couldn't seem to coax a smile. He clutched a lock of her hair for a second, tight, then loosened it to spill free. "Her name was Gail." He said it impatiently, restlessly, as if he were in a hurry to get this over with. "And I don't know how you picked up on it, but yeah, she cheated on me—although the relationship was over long before that. Which I realize now. I don't like what she did, but I'm not tarring her with a feather. I wanted kids, home, security. Standard, ordinary goals. She wanted—needed—something exciting. I was never going to be it. Short and sweet, I bored her."

Samantha opened her mouth. Her first impulse was to reassure him, to violently deny that he could bore any woman. But then she hesitated. It was a heart wound that jerk of a woman had leveled on Seth. Heart wounds didn't heal with words. Words were far too easy to say.

She lifted her hand, and brushed her knuckles across his cheek. The pulse in his throat thumped in response. When she leaned closer, slowly, and whispered a kiss on his lips, he seemed to stop breathing altogether. A shaft of hair swooped over her eyes; she pushed it back, and angled a leg over his as if she could physically pull him to her. He was already aroused, which didn't surprise her. He seemed to have that automatic reaction whenever she was close, but now his manhood came to pulsing life.

Annoyingly she found her hands trembling. She'd certainly volunteered to kiss him before. Maybe he thought those other times that she'd been coming on to him, but that was never true. Physically expressing affection and caring came as naturally to her as breathing, but seducing him had never been on her mind.

It was now. The feelings she had for Seth were as compelling and powerful as any she'd felt for another human being. At times she felt on an empathetic

wavelength with him that plugged straight to her heart.
This was one of those times. That jerkwater broad had
made him feel ordinary, less than exciting, less than a
man. He didn't have to spill out those exact words for
her to hear him. She wanted to make him see that he
was an incredible man. Unbearably exciting. Virile and
sexy and dangerously alluring, far too dangerous for
any woman to resist him.

Communicating that was nothing she had to fake,
since it was exactly how she felt about him. She was
just...scared. She'd loved before, but she'd never been
this painfully, vulnerably in love. She wanted to be the
right woman for him, a woman with enough experience to know what to do, and instead she was just...
herself. A woman with a wholesale history of failure
at reaching a man's heart.

She kissed him again, softly, sweetly, but it wasn't
enough; it wasn't right. She wanted him to believe in
his own magic. Tenderness and tepid kisses were never
going to do that. The risks were just so high in showing him how she really felt. Making love never meant
that he automatically loved her back. It could be, it
could so painfully be, that she'd fallen yet again for a
man who didn't want her in the long term.

But he needed her now.

A silvery reflection caught her eye. She nearly froze
then. From the scarlet velvet drapes to the pedestal
bed, the bedroom had always reminded her of a sultan's bordello, but she hadn't noticed the full-length
standing mirror before. The mirror picked up the
trembling in her hands, her unsure awkwardness when
she climbed on top of him. It was as if the mirror were
watching, a witness to everything she didn't know,
everything she was doing wrong.

And then she forgot the stupid mirror. Seth growled her name in a rough, hoarse whisper. His arms reached up. She must have done something right, because Seth seemed enormously short on control. He pulled her down, down and beneath him. The rush of longing and belonging hit her with shuddering speed. Seth gave her no chance to doubt—none—exactly how he felt about her. She didn't put her faith in magic, but in him.

He loved her. She was sure he'd say it, sure he felt it, and even more sure that he knew they belonged together.

Seth had to face it. He couldn't put it off any longer. He'd never been a coward before, never allowed himself to run from a problem, and damned if he was going to start now.

"So," Samantha said cheerfully, "how do we go about this?"

"You can forget that *we,* buttercup. This is not your problem. It's strictly mine." With his hands on his hips, Seth glared at the offending blue wall. It was time to tear the sucker down.

He'd put it off as long as he could, but everything else in the house was done. The hardwood floors were all sanded and varnished. The kitchen had a face-lift. He'd repaired and replaced the wainscotting in the front hall, redid moldings, painted all over the place. He'd also spent nearly a month in Maine now, and his business in Atlanta couldn't run without a boss forever. If he was going to tear down the damn wall, it had to be this morning, pronto, *now.*

"Just tell me what you plan to do," Samantha said coaxingly.

He shot her a dry glance. She'd used that sweet, feminine innocent tone on him a dozen times in the past weeks, so he was long past buying into *that* nonsense. She was dressed to work, wearing khakis and tennies, a bandanna holding back her hair and size extra-large men's work gloves already on her hands. Jezebel was sitting on the floor, holding a wrench in her mouth. His helpers were ready to wade right in. "Don't *either* of you have anything to do?"

"Not a thing."

"You could both take a nice, long walk on the beach."

"We will. Just a little later," Samantha assured him.

He admired her gall at fibbing right to his face. She was already rolling up her sleeves. He vaguely remembered identifying her as trouble when he'd first laid eyes on her. No question his intuition had been dead on target. He had a hell of a big hickey on his neck. Her doing. Her cheeks still had the blush of a whisker burn from their lovemaking the night before, and he knew damn well her breasts and tush had marks on them, too. Those eyes, that mouth, could incite a man to do incredible, unprincipled, insane things—and had been for the past two weeks.

"You're not getting involved in this," he repeated for—what? The fifth time?

"I was only asking what *you* had to do."

Seth swore she could wear down a saint. "Tear the wall down. Clean up the plaster, put up drywall in the twelve-inch gap, lay a new floor in the open space, then carpet the rest."

"Sounds like fun."

"There's nothing about it that's fun. We're talking filthy, dusty, sweaty work. Now I mean it, Samantha—I'm not letting you near it, and that's that."

"Okay, okay. But—"

"But what?"

"But...are you really, really positive that you want to do this? I mean, what about Jock?"

"Jock, your ghost? Come on, Sam."

"I know you don't like to talk about it, but what if he fixes the wall again? What if this really *is* his room and he doesn't want it fixed? Aren't you at least a little worried after what happened last time?"

"If you think I'm afraid of a ghost, you're dreaming," Seth said firmly.

The wall made him feel uneasy. He was willing to admit that much—at least in the privacy of his mind. But a grown man sure as hell didn't let some damn-fool spookiness stop him from doing something he wanted to. Determinedly he picked up a sledgehammer, made sure Samantha and Jezzie were a safe distance away and then swung back.

The first *thwack* created a satisfyingly fat hole. The second thundering thwack, unfortunately, blocked out the sound of the telephone ringing.

He caught the jangling sound when he swung back again. Naturally the closest receiver was all the way in his bedroom. Before jogging down the hall, though, he pointed a finger at first Samantha, then Jezzie. "Neither of you touch a thing. Not one thing. Stay away from the whole mess."

Two sets of brown eyes expressed wounded feelings at his gruff tone. God, he didn't trust either one of them, but he couldn't get off the telephone that quickly. The call was from Michael. A middle of the day call was rare from his oldest brother, and Seth immediately picked up the tension in Michael's voice. He'd just received his final divorce papers. His "key to freedom," he claimed jovially.

Hell. Seth scalped a hand through his hair. Never mind the faked jovial tone, Michael sounded lower than a well pit and wired. Mike was making old jokes about fitting in the pattern of the Connor men's history of bad luck with women. Seth wanted to say something right, something empathetic and reassuring. But it was tough to give a pep talk to his brother when his own love life was as precarious as a house of cards on the San Andreas Fault.

Michael droned on. He just seemed to need to talk. Seth listened, but when the conversation rambled toward business, his mind inevitably lanced on Samantha.

She'd said she was leaving, but there'd been no more talk of her going anywhere since the first night they made love. Samantha believed herself in love with him. He knew that, felt it every time he touched her, every look she gave him. Staying away was no choice. He couldn't keep his hands off her. In the middle of the night, he found himself dreaming of her, a house in the suburbs, a raggedy herb garden, a brood of dirty-faced urchins wearing crystals with her Cleopatra-dark eyes. Daylight didn't help. He could be working like a dog, and still find himself thinking stupid, embarrassingly romantic things, all focused on her.

But Samantha didn't know how he felt. He hadn't—couldn't—tell her. What happened between their sheets was damn near cataclysmic. He was living with a permanent arousal with her around; his terror of wilting had never happened, and he wanted to feel good about that. He *did* feel good about pleasing her in bed, but the enormous, planet-sized relief at not failing her hadn't lasted long. Not once it sunk in that she had no sexual experience, no basis to compare him with any other guy.

Seth remembered when he lost his virginity. He'd been fifteen. For a short while, he didn't need to eat or sleep. Divide twenty-four hours into minutes, then seconds, and you had eighty-six-thousand, four hundred seconds in a day. Every one of those seconds away from his girl was pure torture. The first throes of hormones were like an endless Christmas. Samantha wasn't fifteen, but it was still new to her the same way. *Nobody* had their judgment on straight when they first discovered sex. Not good sex. Not *real* lovemaking.

His conscience was tangled in guilt. He couldn't leave her in limbo. A good man wouldn't do that to a woman, and it was clearly up to him to fish or cut bait, because Samantha wasn't asking him for anything. She wouldn't. She'd been burned too many times to expect anything from a man. Damnation, she hadn't pushed him even once toward any kind of commitment.

But every time he thought of commitment, a sick, clenched knot of nerves welled in his stomach. She was sunshine to his shadow, effervescent life compared to his quiet ways. She was excitement. He was just an ordinary guy. He'd happened to be there at the right time, to make sure her first foray into physical pleasure was right, safe, secure, positive. But hell, he was kidding himself to think that he was any match for her in the long-term.

"Seth?" Michael's voice snapped his attention back to their phone conversation. "Hell, I didn't realize we'd been on the phone for a half hour. Check with you early next week, okay?"

"Sure," Seth said. They ended the call a few moments later, and Seth promptly jogged back to the blue bedroom.

He stopped in the doorway. Sounds naturally carried down the hall, so he already knew she'd taken a crowbar to the wall. Watching her, though, was something else. She hit like a girl. A lot of style in her swing, the same way female pitchers had style, but absolutely no *oomph.* He shook his head. She couldn't help him tear down walls.

Not physical walls.

Not emotional walls, either, he thought pensively. Whatever had to be done, he had to do himself.

Samantha spotted him. So did his pup. Neither one had the good sense to even look guilty. Seth sighed. "All right, you two. You win. I give up. You wanna go sailing? Rent a boat? Spend an afternoon out on the water?"

"What a *wonderful* idea," Samantha enthused.

"Yeah? Well, when we come back, you both find something else to do. You hear me? That's the deal. You stay out of this whole mess when we get back home. Jezebel?"

Jezzie obediently woofed.

"Samantha?"

"Whatever you say, Connor."

One more afternoon, he thought. He wanted at least one more totally free afternoon with her, just the two of them, even if he knew he was just begging for more heartache.

The whole outing was even worse than he was afraid it would be. It was a day full of sunlight and laughter. Samantha had been sailing before, so she knew what kind of boat to rent, what to do. Jezzie took to the water as if she was half dolphin and a born sailor.

A narrow band of storm clouds clustered on the horizon, but the rain was hours away, and the weather provided enough of a peppery wind to make sailing a challenge. They hugged the shore, skimming the shallows, turning and dipping with the breeze, racing with no one but themselves. Jezzie's fur matted flat against her face in the wind. Samantha tied a blouse over her bathing suit and the sun burned her nose red in spite of the white gunk he made her put on. When she kissed him, she got that gunk all over him. He didn't care. No day could have been more perfect, no woman more perfect than her. Not for him.

They came home, salty, sandy, starved and whipped. Jezebel cleaned out two bowls of food, took her white rabbit outside and crashed on the porch. Seth forayed in the fridge for the makings of dinner, but Samantha stole anything that wasn't tied down. He put her to work making salad, but she ate the makings for that, too, before it ever got into the bowl. Eventually he managed to get her stuffed—no small task. "Shower," she announced right after dinner.

By then, she was talking in one-word sentences and yawning through most of those. She kissed him before she went upstairs—a cheeky, arrogant buss, as if the darn fool woman thought he was actually going to miss her because she'd be out of his sight for a few minutes—and it disgruntled him no end that she was right. It was barely eight o'clock, but Seth doubted she'd make it past the first sitcom.

He cleaned up the kitchen, switched on the tube, found nothing of interest and switched it off again. He'd just decided to head upstairs for a shower himself when he heard her shriek.

Jezebel heard it, too, unlatched the screen door with her mouth and barreled inside and upstairs—right behind Seth. He rounded the corner of the hall and ducked his head into the bathroom. He found scattered towels and a bra hanging from the towel hook and the room steaming with peach shampoo-scented mist—but no Samantha.

"Seth!"

"I'm coming, I'm coming. What's wrong?" He tracked the sound of her voice to the blue bedroom, had the words out of his mouth at the same instant he could *see* what was wrong.

The wall. The damned blue wall. No, they hadn't finished tearing it down that morning, but between his sledgehammer and her crowbar, they'd both taken out huge chunks of plaster. Only those plaster chunks were back in place now, the monster hole fixed, the wall full of patches and cracks but solid. Impossibly solid. All over again.

Samantha just looked at him. "I'm sorry—I didn't really mean to scream. I was just...startled."

She'd wandered into the room by accident, really. She was just walking around while she was towel-drying her hair. A towel was still tucked around her breasts, and another fluffed around her shoulders. When she shook her head, a tumble of damp strands framed her face, and yeah, he could hardly miss the dance of devilment in her eyes.

"I guess there's no help for it. We're down to beating drums and burning black beans, hmm?"

Eleven

———

Every man had his nemesis. Seth could handle snakes, closed-in spaces, fire, heights, and he'd never been squeamish about blood or anything else. Give him a crisis, he always kept his cool. He just really—*really*—didn't like to risk humiliation or embarrassment. That kind of thing slammed straight into his masculine pride.

"Now just bring it up to the room and quit grumbling. What can it hurt?"

Seth had smelled skunk. The noxious fumes from burned black beans weren't worse, but the difference was negligible. Samantha had manufactured a makeshift drum out of chamois cloth strapped to a barrel. She looked silly enough—but not as bad as him, stuck carrying the burned pot.

"Now listen, Seth. You want Jock to move on, don't you? There's no reason to feel funny about this.

Pliny did it. Plutarch did it. We're talking major Roman intellectuals, no lightweights, and they believed this worked. Besides, who's going to ever know we did this but you and me?''

Talk about irrelevant questions, Seth thought glumly. The one woman on earth that he *didn't* want to look like a fool around was her.

"Set the pot on the floor," Samantha ordered.

She didn't have to ask twice. "I don't suppose we could open a window?"

"No." For a few moments she was distracted, juggling the drum, the stick to beat the drum with and the Instruction Book she was paging through at the same time. "Nothing specific about the type of music required," she muttered. "What do you think we should try? A rock-and-roll beat? Two-part rhythm? Or more of an African primitive drumroll?"

"I don't care as long as you don't suggest a sing-along."

"Maybe you should try a reading in the I-Ching while I'm doing this. You know. Combine psychic forces. Eastern, Western, Roman."

Seth cleared his throat. "Now that's a great idea, honey, but I really think we can do without any extra psychic forces."

"Have you ever tried rotating the Chinese iron balls? It's a way of distributing vital energy, unblocking your mind, letting the harmony flow."

"Another great idea," he assured her tactfully, "but we've got so much...um...harmony flowing around here now, that I'm real sure we don't need any more."

Jezebel had taken a powder at the first whiff of the beans. There was just him and her, and damn, was she having fun. It was all a put-on. He thought. He was almost sure. With Samantha, he was never absolutely positive whether she actually believed in hocus-pocus or was just being sassier than the devil. She *did* like to get his goat.

She started a drumbeat. As far as Seth could tell, the rhythm was more reminiscent of Springsteen's "Dancing In The Dark" than anything suited to ghostbusting, but he wasn't about to argue. The sooner they got this over with, the better. Mental film screens rushed through his mind—her zaniness and her sunshine and her whole plucky, sassy approach to life, the way she baby-talked to Jezzie and her love of romantic movies, the way she pushed him over in the middle of the night, stealing the whole bed and wrapped so tight around him that he could hardly move. She was so entwined in his life that he couldn't remember when she wasn't there. And maybe she was doing a good job of exorcising the ghost, but damned if he'd been able to do anything that could exorcise her. Not from his heart.

Eventually—finally—she stopped beating the drums. "Surely that's enough," she said firmly. "Take the sledgehammer to that wall, Seth. Let's give it a try. But I'm sure, quite sure, that if you want to tear down that wall now, you'll be able to. Between the burned beans and the drum—if Jock has a brain in his head—he's surely taken off for Florida by now."

"Ah...Samantha?"

"What?"

"Are you gonna shoot me if I change my mind about that wall?"

Samantha cocked her hands on her hips. "I don't believe it. You made me go through all this, and now you don't want to take down the wall?"

"I didn't want to stop you. Not while you seemed to be having such a good time. But it keeps occurring to me that whoever buys the house could have a passel of kids. Maybe they'll need all the bedrooms. I still think the idea of an upstairs living room is a good one, but maybe the people who buy it will have different ideas. So I'm inclined to leave it alone." He didn't say that he felt uneasy about messing any more with her ghost. It was more than Samantha really seemed to believe. And he didn't want to mess with anything that she believed in.

"So," she said quietly, "you're done then."

"Done?"

She ducked her head and started rolling down her sleeves. "This bedroom was the last project you wanted to do, wasn't it? You finished everything else in the house that you planned to. And I heard you on the telephone a couple of times this week. Sounded like business calls. You must be feeling pushed to go home?"

He'd never mentioned the calls, but he wasn't surprised that she'd picked up on them. "I have to," he admitted. "I can't run my work long-distance forever."

"I understand," she said calmly. "In fact, I've been feeling the same push. It's time I was leaving, too."

He felt as if there was a knife suddenly stabbing his lungs, making it hard for him to breathe, harder yet to talk. She'd said, of course, that she was leaving before. Many times. And there always had to be an end point, a time when they had to separate, but he just wasn't prepared for it at this moment. And Sam...for the first time since he'd known her, she sounded cool and breezy, her tone as practical as common sense. No emotion in sight. He couldn't find anything to say. "Are you...um...planning to continue your ghost hunt?"

A wisp of a smile curved her lips. Just a wisp, as fleeting as mist, then gone. "No. I've had a great time running away, but I've played long enough. I'm going home, too. Hell's bells, I might even take up a disgustingly responsible life-style and put on a business suit. I hate to admit it, but I'm ready."

She untwisted from her coiled position on the floor, and bent over him. Her lips brushed his, softer than the whisker of a rose petal, but her tone was low, fierce. "You've made a difference in my life, Seth. For the first time in my life, I found a man I could trust. I needed you. And you were there. If you regret anything we've done together, I swear I'll come back to haunt you. And you'd better believe it, because that's no idle threat."

"Samantha—"

But she didn't answer him because, that quickly, she walked out of the room. She'd left him with a makeshift drum and a noxious pot of burned beans and the drift, just a drift, of an exotic, erotic perfume. A lump filled his throat as thick and impenetrable as a stone.

There were times when a woman had to be tough. Maybe fifty years from now, Samantha could try to feel proud for the way she'd handled this.

Her bags were packed. So were his. Her Firebird was gassed up, oiled, freshly washed. So was his truck. The last load of laundry was out of the dryer, his separated from hers. She was still missing a pair of tiger-print underpants, but she'd given up looking. Upstairs now, Jezebel trailing on her heels and getting impossibly underfoot, she went from room to room latching windows and doors and making sure the lights were shut off.

"All done up here," she said when she came back downstairs. "What's left?"

Seth was at the sink, rinsing the last of the breakfast dishes. Pancakes. He'd made a million, and she'd barely managed to swallow even one. "Haven't touched anything in the refrigerator yet. And I have to deal with the trash and lock up. That's about it."

"I'll do the food." She opened the fridge. Her voice was as cheerful as birdsong. Peppy. No telltale clue how she felt. Her crystal dangled between her breasts, right over the spot where last night, Seth had given her an intimate rough love bite. Both of them had been wild the night before, their lovemaking a coming together like the force of two hurricane winds. And later, in the wee hours of the morning, there'd been a second time, slow, desperate, a spilling of hopeless, helpless loving emotions.

At least she'd felt that desperation. A clean break was the only way she was going to survive this, Samantha knew. It shouldn't have been a surprise that he didn't love her. It just hurt. Hurt like the burn and sear of fire. Seth had so much love in him, and the right woman should have, would have, been able to coax him to take down those walls.

She poured out the milk, disposed of the soda pop. "I don't suppose we have a box anywhere? Some kind of carton? We still have flour, sugar, some canned goods. I don't know what to do with them."

"I'll find a box. Take whatever you can use, and I'll stash the rest in the back of the truck."

All the little details of closing the house were finally done. Leaving together struck Samantha as a good idea, which was the only reason she'd stayed last night. She didn't want him to have to close up the house alone. She didn't want him to have to *be* alone, spending the yawning long hours of the night by himself.

"Well, that's it." She swung her purse strap to her shoulder, and then crouched down to Jezebel. "Can I have a kiss, baby? I'm gonna miss you more than you know."

Jezebel not only kissed her, but enthusiastically drooled all over her coral blouse. Seth fussed, but Samantha—how many times did she have to tell him?—didn't care. She adored his pup. Hurriedly, though, she stood up. She just wanted on and out with this now. "You've got the key to the front door?"

"Yeah."

The three of them traipsed outside at the same time. Samantha heard the heavy lock click in the oak door, heard it straight in the knell of her chest. By contrast, it was a daffodil-spring kind of morning. The sun was blindingly bright, the gulls screaming and the waves splish-splashing on the shore. She glanced at the tall white lighthouse, then quickly away.

"Okay. No long, drawn-out, corny goodbye scenes. I want a kiss and a hug and that's it." She took a kiss and a hug, not looking at his face. She'd taken care, infinitely great care, not to look directly into his eyes all morning, and her heart was pounding too hard and too loudly to even notice his hand suddenly clutch her shoulder. She spun around and climbed down the porch steps. Jezebel tried to tangle in front of her.

"No, baby, you stay with Seth. You're going for a ride in the truck."

Her sandals sank like sponges in the grass as she crossed the driveway. She opened the car door, tossed in her purse, and rolled down the window. She had the bad, bad feeling that she was going to cry and cry hard. She just didn't want to do it until she was out of sight and down the road.

She slipped into the seat, strapped on the seat belt and turned the key. The Firebird engine obediently roared. She put the gearshift into reverse and glanced in the rearview mirror. Thank heavens she did. Jezebel had chosen to locate smack dab in the middle of the driveway, blocking the path, her tongue lolling and her tail wagging. "Seth, call Jezzie!"

"No."

Samantha blinked. She wasn't expecting to hear a "no." She also wasn't expecting to see him suddenly stride toward her faster than a bear with a fire on his tail. He yanked open the driver's door. "Come out of there, Sam."

"Why?"

He didn't answer her, just reached in—bumped his head—and snapped her free from the safety harness. "I know you have to go. But you're not leaving yet. I'll be damned if I'll let you leave yet."

"Why?" She didn't mean to sound like a broken record, but his sudden change in behavior was totally unlike Seth.

"Because I love you. That's why. I already know it won't work. I would never want to pin you down. It'd be like trying to cage a ray of sunshine or trapping a butterfly. I want kids and a house in the suburbs and just a plain, quiet, ordinary life. So we want different things. So it won't work. But that sure as hell doesn't mean I don't love you more than life."

Sometime, soon, her lungs had to remember that fancy trick about exhaling. All the air felt trapped in her chest. She couldn't breathe for a prayer or a song. "You do?"

"Yeah, I do. *Love* you. And you're not going anywhere until I'm sure you believe that."

Even before she was halfway out of the car, his hands clenched around her upper arms and he kissed her. There was no room. They were both mangled between their bodies and the open car door and Jezebel, who easily figured out there was action going on that she wanted in on. Yet his lips fused on hers, that's all she knew, in a taking and a giving all at once, fierce, angry, so wild, so... soft.

It wouldn't take much, she thought, for both of them to go up in smoke. It never had. Yet no matter how liquid he made her feel, she forced herself to pull back from his kiss. Not far. For the price of her heart, she couldn't have moved any farther from him than the distance it took to see his face. "Seth. Where did you get the idea that I didn't want plain, ordinary things?"

"Come on, Sam. You know."

Actually she didn't. Searching his eyes, she still didn't. "I like... excitement. The excitement of a bonfire on a beach. Or a walk in the woods, discovering wildflowers and trees and everything in life. Or making love with a man who sets me on fire. That's excitement. That's the kind of things we've done together from the beginning. Where did you get the idea that I wanted something else?"

The pad of his thumb traced her lower lip, as if memorizing the texture of the mouth he'd just kissed. "Honey, I'm never going to be more than a carpenter. And I'm not an imaginative man. Not the kind of guy to think up romantic things. The things you like, the things you need."

"You're out of your mind. We made love in a lighthouse, Connor. We nearly went crazy in the middle of this yard one midnight. Romantic doesn't have to be a dozen roses with a florist tag. It's what two people feel together, what they bring each other."

"Maybe. But..." The muscle suddenly tensed in his jaw. "Samantha, there's something you don't know." He hesitated, his gaze suddenly sharp on her face. He couldn't seem to get the words out, but then he tried again. "I'm afraid."

"Not of me."

"Yeah, of you. Of failing you. That's the reason I never said anything, the reason I held back for so long. And it's nothing I want to tell you now, except that I can't let you believe I would just walk out of your life without a hell of a good reason." He spit out the rest. "I told you I was involved before. Well, a woman doesn't cheat on a lover, not if he was doing anything right. Not if she was satisfied. And after that, I had a run-in with some real proof that I was more than capable of being a real failure in that department."

"Oh, Seth. That's what was haunting you all this time?"

"There wasn't a problem. Not with you. But dammit, Sam, you could just as easily have gotten bored with me. You're the most sensual, passionate woman I've ever known. And I'll sure as hell never be more than me."

"So, you were afraid of disappointing me as a lover?" She kicked the car door closed. He didn't answer her. He'd gotten it out, what he could say, all he could say, and maybe even more than Seth had thought he'd ever tell her. A memory flickered through her mind, of his sputtering cough when she told him the old folklore about ginseng tea being an aphrodisiac. She'd thought his reaction was funny then, a response of humor to an old-time myth. She didn't think it was funny now.

What he'd been worried about was no myth, and the look in his eyes was as naked as pride. A man's pride, raw and exposed, and there was a man's vulnerability in his mouth, his eyes, the stillness in his whole body. Lord, how on earth could she find the right words to say?

"You're still afraid it could happen, aren't you?"

"Hell, yes."

"Well, I think it could, too." *That* brought his head up. "I think there are probably going to be times when I fail you. Badly. Painfully. I don't know much about making a relationship work. So far, I've only been good at screwing them up. You'd have to be patient. I have a lot to learn."

"Sweetheart, you don't have a damn thing to learn about loving."

"The heck I don't. If you take me, Connor, your eyes had better be open about all my faults. They've sure daunted other men. You think I'm not terrified of failing you?"

He looked at her—one of *those* looks—as if what she were saying was so impossible that she couldn't conceivably be operating on all pistons. "Honey—"

"I think that's what loving is about. Finding the one person where it's okay. You can do stupid things, you can make mistakes, you can fail. You can be... yourself. And it's still okay, because you know, you trust, that the person you love is still going to be there. They *want* to be there, not just for the good times, but for the rough times as well." She hesitated. "At least ... that's how I feel about you."

She wasn't sure, until that instant, if anything she said had gotten through. He didn't move for a flicker of a second. He didn't even seem to be breathing. But then he pounced. In the dizzying spin of a moment, he crushed her so tightly in his arms that the drumbeat of his heart was inseparable from her own, and when he took her mouth... Oh, Lord, that kiss. It was like a direct call from his soul to hers, a promise and a vow all at once, and the power and terror of love was laid right on the line.

"I love you, Samantha Adams," he whispered. "I love you just that way. For the rest of our lives, I want to be there for you, through thick and thin, no matter what happens. And I swear I'll do my best to make you happy."

She had no doubts about that. But heavens, what a job she had cut out for her. His confidence in himself, in his prowess as a man and a lover, needed building. It would take time. Maybe an entire lifetime, if she was to make him feel as incredible, as infinitely special, as she saw him as a man.

There was a time she would have believed she wasn't up for the job. For so long she'd felt...unlovable. Too difficult, too inadequate, too *something* for anyone to really love her. But that was before Seth. Before she'd found the one man who accepted her, exactly as she was, for herself alone.

Well, he'd just have to pay, she thought fleetingly. There was a price for his loving her. He was stuck with her. Stuck like glue. She considered the long hours in bed, the years and hours of making love, that it could take to further his confidence in himself as a lover.

She pushed at the buttons of his tattersall shirt. Might as well, she thought, start as she meant to go on.

"Honey, not here," he murmured. "Anyone could drive in."

That was certainly true. Seth had never believed she had an ounce of practical common sense, when in reality she was aware of a thousand practical things to be done. Setting a time for Seth to meet her parents— heavens, they were going to love him—closing up her Phillie apartment, moving to Atlanta, meeting his brothers. It was all ahead. It all mattered. Just not then.

"Jezebel . . ." She turned her head just far enough to catch the dog's attention. "Watch the driveway. Attack anyone who tries to drive in."

Jezebel woofed agreement.

A curtain stirred in the second-story window. That window, Samantha knew, had been locked, because she'd flipped the latch herself. It was open now, just a crack, and the filmy white lace curtains caught her eye for the briefest second.

Then she forgot it. Seth was catching on. Quickly. Like a match flared in a bed of dry kindling, there was a whoosh and flame of fire in his eyes. When Connor was feeling determined, she was afraid he was as un-budgeable as a rock. He lifted her off the gravel driveway and onto the sunlit grass, but they definitely weren't going to make it as far as the house. Seth was in a mood to please her. She could protest, she could argue, but it was going to happen and that was that

Loving him made her choices easy. She let him have his way.

*   *   *   *   *

That pirate ghost Jock isn't done matchmaking yet. Be sure to look for Michael's story, BEWILDERED, *available in June—from Silhouette Desire.*

▼ SILHOUETTE®

Desire®

MAN of the Month 1994

It's the men you've come
to know and love...
with a bold, new look
that's going to make
you take notice!

January: *SECRET AGENT MAN*
by Diana Palmer

February: *WILD INNOCENCE*
by Ann Major
(next title in her SOMETHING WILD
miniseries)

March: *WRANGLER'S LADY*
by Jackie Merritt
(first title in her SAXON BROTHERS
miniseries)

April: *BEWITCHED*
by Jennifer Greene
(first title in her JOCK'S BOYS
miniseries)

May: *LUCY AND THE STONE*
by Dixie Browning
(next book in her OUTER BANKS
miniseries)

June: *HAVEN'S CALL*
by Robin Elliott

And that's just the first six months! Later in the year, look
for books by Barbara Boswell, Cait London, Joan Hohl,
Annette Broadrick and Lass Small....

MAN OF THE MONTH...ONLY FROM SILHOUETTE DESIRE

MILLION DOLLAR SWEEPSTAKES (III)

No purchase necessary. To enter, follow the directions published. Method of entry may vary. For eligibility, entries must be received no later than March 31, 1996. No liability is assumed for printing errors, lost, late or misdirected entries. Odds of winning are determined by the number of eligible entries distributed and received. Prizewinners will be determined no later than June 30, 1996.

Sweepstakes open to residents of the U.S. (except Puerto Rico), Canada, Europe and Taiwan who are 18 years of age or older. All applicable laws and regulations apply. Sweepstakes offer void wherever prohibited by law. Values of all prizes are in U.S. currency. This sweepstakes is presented by Torstar Corp., its subsidiaries and affiliates, in conjunction with book, merchandise and/or product offerings. For a copy of the Official Rules send a self-addressed, stamped envelope (WA residents need not affix return postage) to: MILLION DOLLAR SWEEPSTAKES (III) Rules, P.O. Box 4573, Blair, NE 68009, USA.

EXTRA BONUS PRIZE DRAWING

No purchase necessary. The Extra Bonus Prize will be awarded in a random drawing to be conducted no later than 5/30/96 from among all entries received. To qualify, entries must be received by 3/31/96 and comply with published directions. Drawing open to residents of the U.S. (except Puerto Rico), Canada, Europe and Taiwan who are 18 years of age or older. All applicable laws and regulations apply; offer void wherever prohibited by law. Odds of winning are dependent upon number of eligibile entries received. Prize is valued in U.S. currency. The offer is presented by Torstar Corp., its subsidiaries and affiliates in conjunction with book, merchandise and/or product offering. For a copy of the Official Rules governing this sweepstakes, send a self-addressed, stamped envelope (WA residents need not affix return postage) to: Extra Bonus Prize Drawing Rules, P.O. Box 4590, Blair, NE 68009, USA.

SWP-S594

IT'S OUR 1000TH SILHOUETTE ROMANCE, AND WE'RE CELEBRATING!

JOIN US FOR A SPECIAL COLLECTION OF LOVE STORIES BY AUTHORS YOU'VE LOVED FOR YEARS, AND NEW FAVORITES YOU'VE JUST DISCOVERED. JOIN THE CELEBRATION...

April
REGAN'S PRIDE by **Diana Palmer**
MARRY ME AGAIN by **Suzanne Carey**

May
THE BEST IS YET TO BE by **Tracy Sinclair**
CAUTION: BABY AHEAD by **Marie Ferrarella**

June
THE BACHELOR PRINCE by **Debbie Macomber**
A ROGUE'S HEART by **Laurie Paige**

July
IMPROMPTU BRIDE by **Annette Broadrick**
THE FORGOTTEN HUSBAND by **Elizabeth August**

SILHOUETTE ROMANCE...VIBRANT, FUN AND EMOTIONALLY RICH! TAKE ANOTHER LOOK AT US! AND AS PART OF THE CELEBRATION, READERS CAN RECEIVE A FREE GIFT!

YOU'LL FALL IN LOVE ALL OVER AGAIN WITH SILHOUETTE ROMANCE!

Silhouette®
™

CEL1000

Rugged and lean...and the best-looking,
sweetest-talking men to be found in the
entire Lone Star state!

Diana Palmer

LONG, TALL TEXANS

In July 1994, Silhouette is very proud to bring you
Diana Palmer's first three LONG, TALL TEXANS.
CALHOUN, JUSTIN and TYLER—the three cowboys
who started the legend. Now they're back by popular
demand in one classic volume—and they're ready to
lasso your heart! Beautifully repackaged for this
special event, this collection is sure to be a
longtime keepsake!

"Diana Palmer makes a reader want to find a Texan
of her own to love!"   —*Affaire de Coeur*

**LONG, TALL TEXANS—the first three—
reunited in this special roundup!**

**Available in July,
wherever Silhouette books are sold.**